The Conqueror

Being The True And Romantic Story Of Alexander Hamilton

Book III

by

Gertrude Atherton

Double 9 BOOKS

The Conqueror

Being The True And Romantic Story Of Alexander Hamilton

Book III

by Gertrude Atherton

ISBN: 978-93-73407-02-9

Published by

DOUBLE 9 BOOKS

2/13-B, Ansari Road
Daryaganj, New Delhi – 110002
info@double9books.com
www.double9books.com
Tel. 011-40042856

ABOUT THE AUTHOR

During the whole literary journey, Gertrude Atherton wrote over 40 novels, several short stories and genuine essays ended up with a successful career. She was majorly known for her prolific contribution to literature during the late 19th century. Born in 1857, she grew up and brought up in San Francisco California in a wealthy and socially stable family. In both countries, the United States and Europe, she completed her education with a vivid understanding of a broad cultural base. She wrote epic genres including novels and short stories and essays. Wide predictions and explanations of diverse themes and styles helped her to become notable at a rapid pace. She often dived into the social and cultural norms of her time and staggered critiques of society. Atherton was well known for her collaboration and association with the greatest literary figures of her time which includes H.G Wells and Ambrose Bierce. However, her popularity slowed down during the 20th century and her interest in her work was acknowledged by her peers and most of her scholars appreciated her for her major contribution to American literature.

CONTENTS

BOOK III THE LITTLE LION

CHAPTER I 7
CHAPTER II 11
CHAPTER III 19
CHAPTER IV 22
CHAPTER V 29
CHAPTER VI 34
CHAPTER VII 41
CHAPTER VIII 46
CHAPTER IX 50
CHAPTER X 53
CHAPTER XI 56
CHAPTER XII 63

BOOK III
THE LITTLE LION

CHAPTER I

Hamilton's body succumbed to the climax of Trenton and Princeton upon months of hardship and exposure, and he was in hospital for a week with a rheumatic fever. But Troup, whose exchange had been effected, was with him most of the time, and his convalescence was made agreeable by many charming women. He was not the only brilliant young man in the army, for Troup, Fish, Burr, Marshall, were within a few months or, at most, a year or two of his age, and there were many others; men had matured early in that hot period before the Revolution, when small boys talked politics, and even the women thought of little else; but Hamilton, through no fault of his, had inspired his friends with the belief that he was something higher than human, and they never tired of sounding his praises. Moreover, Washington had not hesitated to say what he thought of him, and the mere fact that he had won the affection of that austere Chieftain was enough to give him celebrity. At all events, he was a dazzling figure, and pretty women soothed many a weary hour. As for Troup, who was unpleasantly anatomical, he had a fresh story for every day of the horrors of the prison cattle-ship *Mentor*, where half the prisoners had died of filth, starvation, and fever, from putrid water and brutal treatment.

But never was there a more impatient invalid than Hamilton. He was astonished and disgusted that his body should defy his mind, and at the first moment possible he was up and about his duties with the army at Morristown. Troup was ordered to join the army under Gates in the North.

Morristown was a natural fortress, a large fertile valley, protected by precipitous hills and forests, yet with defiles known to the Americans, through which they could retreat if necessary. It was within striking distance of New Brunswick and Amboy, in which towns Washington kept the British cooped up for months, not permitting them to cut a stick of forest wood without fighting for it. "Here was seen," to quote Hamilton, "the spectacle of a powerful army straitened within narrow limits by the phantom of a military force, and never permitted to transgress those limits with impunity; in which skill supplied the place of means, and disposition was the substitute for an army."

Congress had invested Washington with such extraordinary powers after the brilliant exploit at Trenton, that in Europe he was called "The Dictator of America." Therein lay the sole cause of the ultimate victory of the Revolutionists, and had the States been more generous, and less jealous of delegating powers to Congress, he would have driven out the British in short order.

Mrs. Washington had joined her General—she kept an eye on him—at Freeman's Tavern, which had been converted into comfortable headquarters, and he was happy in his military family: Colonel Harrison, indefatigable and fearless, affectionately known as "Old Secretary"; Tench Tilghman of Maryland, young, accomplished, cheerful, devoted to Washington and serving without pay, for his fortune was considerable; Richard Kidder Meade, sprightly, enthusiastic, always willing to slave; and John Fitzgerald,—all in an attitude of perpetual adoration. But he lacked a secretary of the requisite ability, and as soon as he heard of Hamilton's return to camp he sent for him.

Hamilton was feeling almost well, and he walked rapidly across the village green to headquarters, delighted at the prospect of seeing Washington again. He had acquired a military air and walked more erectly than ever, for he was somewhat sensitive of his juvenile appearance. He found Washington in a front room on the second floor. The General wore his usual blue and buff, and looked less harassed and worn than when he had last seen him. He rose and shook hands warmly with Hamilton, who thanked him again for the messages he had received while in hospital.

"I would have had you brought here if there had been any place to make you comfortable; and I am going to ask you to come and live with me now—as my aide and secretary."

Hamilton sprang to his feet impetuously. "Oh, sir!" he exclaimed, "I don't want to leave the regular line of promotion! I don't want to leave my men. I'm much attached to them. And I'll not deny my ambition, sir; I want opportunities to distinguish myself. I've already refused two generals. This war will last for years. There is no reason in the world why I should not be a general in three."

"No," said Washington, "there is none; there is every possibility of your becoming one of the most brilliant figures on the revolutionary battlefields. I admit that, and I understand your ambition. Nevertheless, I think I can prove to you that there is another way in which you can serve your country better. I know your uncompromising sense of duty and your high patriotism, and I am sure you will accept my invitation when I prove to you that while there are hundreds to fight valorously, even brilliantly, there is scarcely a man I can get to write my letters who can do more than punctuate properly or turn a sentence neatly. You must know the inexpressible value of a brilliant accomplished versatile secretary, with a brain capable of grasping every question that arises—and you can imagine how many of that sort have come my way. I have been driven nearly distracted, dictating, explaining, revising—when I have so much else to think of. Besides the constant correspondence with the Congress and the States, something else is always turning up—to-day it is the exchange of prisoners, a most important and delicate matter. Were you my secretary, you would also be my brain: a word would be sufficient. I could trust you so implicitly that if matters pressed I could confidently sign my name to whatever you wrote without reading it over. There is no one else living of whom I can say that. You are the most useful young man in America, and if you will give your great brain to this country from this time on, she will be far more grateful to you than if you merely continued to fight, splendidly as you have done that. And *I* need you—I have no words to tell you how much."

"Sir," said Hamilton, deeply touched, "no human being could withstand such an appeal, and your words of praise are glory enough. I will come as soon as you say, and do the best I can."

"Come at once. The British persist in treating us as rebels. It is for you, with your inspired pen, to force and coax them to regard us with the respect an educated thinking people—not a horde of ignorant rebels, as they imagine—deserve. If you do that, you will do a greater service to your country than if you rose to be first in military rank. Here are some notes. When you have finished, write to Congress and ask for the rank of Lieutenant-Colonel; and move up here to-day, if possible. I cannot tell you how happy I shall be to have you a member of my family."

Washington had won his point. A shrewd judge of men, he had calculated upon Hamilton succumbing to an appeal to his sense of patriotic duty—the strongest passion in his passionate nature. Much as he loved Hamilton, he had no hesitation in using him, and our petted young hero was to learn what work meant for the first time in his life. He wrote most of the day, often half the night; but although he chafed angrily at the confinement, beat many a tattoo on the floor with his heels, and went for a hard ride more than once that he might keep his temper, the result was that mass of correspondence, signed "George Washington," which raised the commander of the American forces so high in the estimation of Europe, adding to his military renown the splendour of a profound and luminous intellect.

There was, also, some correspondence with the Congress regarding the disposition of his artillery men. He insisted upon definite provision for them, and they were permitted to enlist in the Continental Army. They loved him, and the final parting on March 18th, with cannon as well as men!—made him ill for half a day.

Otherwise his life at Headquarters was very pleasant Tilghman and Meade became two of the most congenial friends he ever made. The tavern was comfortable, and he had a room to himself for a time. The dining room reunions were agreeable in spite of their formality. Besides the amiable military family, and the most motherly of women, who knit him stockings and kept his wardrobe in order, there were frequent visitors. The Livingston girls were spending the winter with their aunt, Lady Sterling, and, with their beautiful cousin, the Lady Kitty Alexander, often drove over to a five o'clock dinner or the more informal supper. The Boudinots and Morgans, the generals in camp at Morristown and their wives, and the more distinguished officers, were frequently dined at Headquarters. Washington sat halfway in the table's length, with Mrs. Washington opposite. Hamilton was placed at the head of the table on the day of his arrival, a seat he retained while a member of the family. The Chief encouraged him to talk, and it must be confessed that he talked from the time he sat down till the meal finished. His ideas were always on the rush, and talking was merely thinking aloud. As he expressed himself with wit and elegance, and on subjects which interested them all profoundly, illuminating everything he touched, old men and young would lean forward and listen with respect to the wisdom of a young man who was yet an infant in the eyes of the law. How he escaped being insufferably spoiled can only be explained by the ceaseless activity of his brain, and the fact that the essence of which prigs are made was not in him. That he was utterly without commonplace conceit is indisputable, for he was the idol of the family. Harrison christened him "The Little Lion," a name his friends used for their aptest designation as long as he lived, and assumed a paternal relation which finished only with the older man's death. The Lady-in-chief made such a pet of him that he was referred to in the irreverent Tory press as "Mrs. Washington's Tom-cat."

"Alexander," said Kitty Livingston to him, one day, "have a care. You are too fortunate. The jealous gods will smite you."

But Hamilton, thinking of those terrible months in the previous year, of mental anxiety and physical hardship, when, in bitter weather, he had often gone hungry and insufficiently clothed, and of his present arduous duties, concluded there was a fine balance in his affairs which doubtless would placate the gods.

CHAPTER II

In May and July there were illustrious additions to Washington's family,—John Laurens and Lafayette. Both became the intimate friends of Hamilton, the former one of the few passionate attachments of his life. Although Hamilton was by no means indifferent to the affection he inspired in nine-tenths of the people he met, he did not himself love easily. He was too analytical, he saw people too precisely as they were, and his acquaintance with human nature had made him too cynical to permit the flood gates of his affections to open except under uncommon stress. He dreaded disappointment. For Troup, Fish, Stevens, Meade, and Tilghman he had a deep affection and served their interests ardently; for Washington a contradictory budget of emotions, which were sometimes to be headed "respectful affection," at others "irritated resentment," now and again a moment of adoration. While he could not pay sufficient tribute to Washington's magnanimity and generosity, he had by now seen him in too many tempers, had been ground too fine in his greedy machine, to think on him always with unqualified enthusiasm. Lafayette, brilliant, volatile, accomplished, bubbling with enthusiasm for the cause of Liberty, and his own age within a few months, he liked sincerely and always. There was no end to the favours he did him, and Lafayette loved no one better in his long and various career. Women, Hamilton fancied sharply and forgot quickly.

But Laurens, the "young Bayard of the Revolution," fresh from the colleges and courts of Europe, a man so handsome that, we are told, people experienced a certain shock when he entered the room, courtly, accomplished to the highest degree, of flawless character, with a mind as noble and elevated as it was intellectual, and burning with the most elevated patriotism,—he took Hamilton by storm, capturing judgement as well as heart, and loving him as ardently in return.

Like Hamilton, Laurens was of Huguenot descent; he was born in South Carolina, of a distinguished family. Against the expressed wish of his father he had returned to America, made his way to Headquarters and offered his services to Washington, who immediately attached him to his military household. The unhappiest of men, praying for death on every battlefield, he lived long enough to distinguish himself by a bravery so reckless, by such startling heroic feats, that he was, beyond all question, the popular young hero of the Revolution. He worshipped Washington as one might worship a demi-god, and risked his life for him on two occasions. But Hamilton was the friend of his life; the bond between them was romantic and chivalrous. Each burned to prove the strength of his affection, to sacrifice himself for the other. Laurens slaved at Washington's less important correspondence, and Hamilton's turn came later. The age has passed for such friendships; but at that time, when young men were nurtured on great ideas, when they were sacrificing themselves in a sacred cause, and had seen next to nothing of the frivolities of life, they were understandable enough.

Hamilton was obliged to share his room with both the young men, and they slept on three little cots in a small space. When the nights were insufferably hot they would go out and lie on the grass and talk until they were in a condition to sleep anywhere. Hamilton would forecast the next movement of the enemy; Laurens and Lafayette would tell all they knew about military science in Europe; and then they would discuss the future of the liberated country and the great ideals which must govern her. And when men can be idealistic while fighting the Jersey mosquito, it must be admitted that they are of the stuff to serve their country well.

But all this delightful intercourse was interrupted in August. Washington gave battle to the British at Brandywine, was defeated, and in the following month surprised them at Germantown, and was defeated again. Nevertheless, he had astonished the enemy with his strength and courage so soon after a disastrous battle. To hold Philadelphia was impossible, however, and the British established themselves in the Capital of the colonies, making, as usual, no attempt to follow up their victories.

Washington went into temporary quarters near the village of Whitemarsh. His own were in a baronial hall at the head of a beautiful valley. Old trees shaded the house, and a spring of pure water bubbled in a fountain before the door. The men were encamped on the hills at the north.

There was a great hall through the centre of the mansion, and here Washington held his audiences and councils of war. The house throughout was of extreme elegance, and much to the taste of the younger members of the family, particularly of Hamilton, who spent the greater part of his leisure in the library. But his enjoyment of this uncommon luxury was brief.

Washington must have reinforcements or his next engagement might be his last. There was but one source from which he could obtain a considerable supply, and that was from the army of Gates in the North. But Gates was swollen with the victory of Saratoga and the capture of Burgoyne, and was suspected to be in the thick of an intrigue to dethrone Washington and have himself proclaimed Commander-in-chief. At the moment he was the idol of the army, and of the northern and eastern States, for his victories were tangible and brilliant, while Washington's surer processes were little appreciated. Therefore to get troops from him would be little less difficult than to get them from Lord Howe, short of a positive command, and this prerogative Washington did not think it politic to use. He called a council of war, and when it was over he went to his private office and sent for Alexander Hamilton.

He looked haggard, as if from sleepless nights, and for a moment after Hamilton entered the room, although he waved his hand at a chair, he stared at him without speaking. Hamilton divined what was coming—he attended all councils of war—and sat forward eagerly. The prospect of a holiday from clerical work would alone have filled him with youth, and he knew how great a service he might be able to render the cowering Republic.

"Hamilton," said Washington, finally, "you are as much in my secret thoughts as I am myself. If I attempted to deceive you, you would divine what I withheld. It is a relief to speak frankly to you, I dare not demand these troops from Gates, because there is more than a possibility he would defy me, and that the Congress and a large part of the army would sustain him. He has given sufficient evidence of his temper in sending me no official notice of the battle of Saratoga. But unless I am to meet with overwhelming disaster here, I must have reinforcements. It may be possible to extract these by diplomacy, and I have selected you for the mission, because I feel sure that you will not forget the issues at stake for a moment, because you never lose your head, and because you will neither be overawed by Gates's immediate splendour, nor will you have any young desire to assert the authority which I give you as a last resort. There is another point: If you find that Gates purposes to employ his troops on some expedition, by the prosecution of which the common cause will be more benefited than by their being sent down to reinforce this army, you must suspend your consideration for me. God knows I am tender of my reputation, and I have no wish to be disgraced, but we are or should be fighting for a common cause and principle, and should have little thought of individual glory. However, I do not believe in the disinterestedness of Gates, nor in his efficiency on a large scale. But I leave everything in your hands."

Hamilton stood up, his chest rising, and stared at his Chief.

"Sir," he said, after a moment, "do you appreciate that you are placing your good name and your future in my hands?" For a moment he realized that he was not yet of age.

"You are the only being to whom I can confide them, and who can save this terrible situation."

"And you have the magnanimity to say that if Gates has a chance of other victories to let him go unhindered?" He had one of his moments of adoration and self-abnegation for this man, whose particular virtues, so little called upon in ordinary affairs, gave him so lonely a place among men.

Washington jerked his head. There was nothing more to say. Hamilton's head dropped for a moment, as if he felt the weight of an iron helmet, and his lips moved rapidly.

"Are you saying your prayers when your lips work like that?" asked Washington, crossly.

Hamilton threw back his head with a gay laugh. His eyes were sparkling, his nostrils dilating; his whole bearing was imperious and triumphant. "Never mind that. I'll undertake this mission gladly, sir, and I think I'll not fail. My old friend Troup is his aide. He will advise me of many things. I'll bring you back those regiments, sir. One way or another a thing can always be managed."

The light in Hamilton's face was reflected on Washington's. "You are my good genius," he said shortly. "Take care of yourself. You will have to ride hard, for there is no time to lose, but be careful not to take cold. I shall give you orders in writing. Come back as soon as you can. I believe I am not lacking in courage, but I always have most when you are close by."

There is a print somewhere representing Hamilton setting forth on this mission. He is mounted on a handsome white horse, and wears a long green cloak, one end thrown over a shoulder. His three-cornered hat is pulled low over his eyes. In the rear is an orderly.

He started on the 30th of October, riding hard through the torn desolate country, toward Newburg on the Hudson. He was three days making the distance, although he snatched but a few hours' rest at night, and but a few moments for each meal. From Newburg he crossed to Fishkill and, acting on his general instructions, ordered Putnam to despatch southward three brigades; and on his own account despatched seven hundred Jersey militia on the same expedition.

He then started hot and hard for Albany, a dangerous as well as exhausting journey, for neither savage tribes nor redcoats could be far in the distance. His mental anxiety by now wore as severely as the physical strain. None knew better than he that his talents were not for diplomacy. He was too impatient, too imperious, too direct for its sinuous methods. On the other hand, he had a theory that a first-rate mind could, for a given time, be bent in any direction the will commanded, and he had acquired an admirable command of his temper. But the responsibility was terrific, and he was half ill when he reached Albany. He presented himself at General Gates's headquarters at once.

Gates, like Lee, was a soldier of fortune; and low-born, vain, weak, and insanely ambitious. He had been advised of Hamilton's coming, and had no intention of giving Washington an opportunity to rival his own achievements and reëstablish himself with the army and the Congress. He received Hamilton surrounded by several of his military family; and for the first time our fortunate hero encountered in high places active enmity and dislike. He had incurred widespread jealousy on account of his influence over Washington, and for the important part he was playing in national affairs. To the enemies of the Commander-in-chief he represented that exalted personage, and was particularly obnoxious. Never was a youth in a more difficult position.

"I cannot expose the finest arsenal in America," said Gates, pompously, "to the possibility of destruction. Sir Henry Clinton may return at any minute. Nor could I enterprise against Ticonderoga were my army depleted. Nor can I leave the New England States open to the ravages and the depredations of the enemy."

These statements made no impression on Hamilton, and he argued brilliantly and convincingly for his object, but Gates was inflexible. He would send one brigade and no more.

Hamilton retired, uneasy and dejected. Gates had an air of omnipotence, and his officers had not concealed their scorn. He hesitated to use his authority, for a bold defiance on the part of Gates might mean the downfall of Washington, perhaps of the American cause. That Washington was practically the American army, Hamilton firmly believed. If he fell, it was more than likely that the whole tottering structure would crumble.

Another reason inclined him not to press Gates too far. He had been able to order seventy-seven hundred troops from Fishkill, which was more than Washington had expected, although by no means so many as he needed. He therefore wrote to the Chief at length, sent for Troup, and threw himself on the bed; he was well-nigh worn out.

Troup was already in search of him, and met the messenger. Big and bronzed, bursting with spirits, he seemed to electrify the very air of the room he burst into without ceremony. Hamilton sat up and poured out his troubles.

"You have an affinity for posts of danger," said Troup. "I believe you to be walking over a powder-mine here. I am not in their confidence, for they know what I think of Washington, but I believe there is a cabal on foot, and that Gates may be in open rebellion any minute. But he's a coward and a bully. Treat him as such. Press your point and get your troops. He is but the tool of a faction, and I doubt if they could make him act when it came to the point. He wants to make another grand coup before striking. Look well into what regiment he gives you. Which are you to have?"

"General Patterson's."

"I thought as much. It is the weakest of the three now here, consists of but about six hundred rank and file fit for duty. There are two hundred militia with it, whose time of service is so near expiring that they will have dissolved ere you reach Headquarters."

Hamilton had sprung to his feet in a fury. He forgot his pains, and let his temper fly with satisfaction in the exercise. "If that is the case," he cried, when he had finished his anathema of Gates, "I'll have the men;" and he dashed at his writing materials. But he threw his pen aside in a moment. "I'll wait till to-morrow for this. I must be master of myself. Tell me of Saratoga. You distinguished yourself mightily, and no one was more glad than I."

Troup talked while Hamilton rested. That evening he took him to call at the Schuyler mansion, high on the hill.

Philip Schuyler was the great feudal lord of the North. He had served the colonial cause in many ways, and at the outbreak of the Revolution had been one of its hopes and props. But brilliant as his exploits had been, the intrigues of Gates, after the fall of Ticonderoga, had been successful, and he was deprived of the army of the North before the battle of Saratoga. The day of exoneration came, but at present he was living quietly at home, without bitterness. A man of the most exalted character, he drew added strength from adversity, to be placed at the service of the country the moment it was demanded. Mrs. Schuyler, herself a great-granddaughter of the first patroon, Killian Van Rensselaer, was a woman of strong character, an embodied type of all the virtues of the Dutch pioneer housewife. She had a lively and turbulent family of daughters, however, and did not pretend to manage them. The spirit of our age is feeble and bourgeois when compared with the independence and romantic temper of the stormy days of this Republic's birth. Liberty was in the air; there was no talk but of freedom and execration of tyrants; young officers had the run of every house, and Clarissa Harlowe was the model for romantic young "females." Angelica Schuyler, shortly before the battle of Saratoga, had run off with John Barker Church, a young Englishman of distinguished connections, at present masquerading under the name of Carter; a presumably fatal duel having driven him from England. Subsequently, both Peggy and Cornelia Schuyler climbed out of windows and eloped in a chaise and four, although there was not an obstacle worth mentioning to union with the youths of their choice. It will shock many good mothers of the present day to learn that all these marriages were not only happy, but set with the brilliance of wealth and fashion. When Hamilton was introduced to the famous white hall of the Schuyler mansion on the hill, Cornelia and Peggy were still free in all but fancy; Elizabeth, by far the best behaved, was the hope of Mrs. Schuyler's well-regulated soul and one of the belles of the Revolution. Hamilton was enchanted with her, although his mind was too weighted for love. Her spirits were as high as his own, and they talked and laughed until midnight as gaily as were Gates's army marching south. But Hamilton was a philosopher; nothing could be done before the morrow; he might as well be happy and forget. He had met many clever and accomplished American women by this, and Lady Kitty Alexander and Kitty and Susan Livingston were brilliant. He had also met Angelica Church, or Mrs. Carter, as she was called, one of the cleverest and most high-spirited women of her time. It had crossed his mind that had she been free, he might have made a bold dash for so fascinating a creature, but it seemed to him to-night that on the whole he preferred her sister. "Betsey" Schuyler had been given every advantage of education, accomplishment, and constant intercourse with the best society in the land. She had skill and tact in the management of guests, and without; being by any means a woman of brilliant parts, understood the questions of the day; her brain was informed with shrewd common sense. Hamilton concluded that she was quite clever enough, and was delighted with her beauty, her charm of manner, and style. Her little figure was graceful and distinguished, her complexion the honey and claret that artists extol, and she had a pair of big black eyes which were alternately roguish, modest, tender, sympathetic; there were times when they were very lively, and even suggested a temper. She was bright without attempting to be witty, but that she was deeply appreciative of wit Hamilton had soothing cause to know. And he had learned from the admiring Troup that she was as intrepid as she was wholly and daintily feminine. Altogether, Hamilton's fate was sealed when he bent over her hand that night, although he was far from suspecting it, so heavily did duty press the moment he was alone in his rooms.

On the following morning he asked for an interview with General Schuyler and several other military men whom he knew to be friendly to Washington, and they confirmed the advice of Troup. In the afternoon he wrote to Gates a letter that was peremptory, although dignified and circumspect, demanding the addition of a superior brigade. He expressed his indignation in no measured terms, and in more guarded phrases his opinion of the flimsiness of the victorious General's arguments. Gates sent the troops at once, and despatched a volume of explanation to Washington.

Hamilton set out immediately for New Windsor, Troup bearing him company the greater part of the way, for he was feeling very ill. But he forgot his ailments when he arrived. To his fury he discovered that not a regiment had gone south. Two of the brigades, which had received no pay for eight months, had mutinied, and he was obliged to ask Governor Clinton to borrow $5000, with which to pay them off. He had the satisfaction of despatching them, wrote a peremptory letter to Putnam, who had other plans brewing, another to Gates, asking for further reinforcements, then went to bed in Governor Clinton's house with fever and rheumatism. But he wrote to Washington, apprising him of a scheme among the officers of the northern department to recover the city of New York, and denouncing Putnam in the most emphatic terms. Two days later he recovered sufficiently to proceed to Fishkill, where he wrested troops from Putnam, and ascertained that heavy British reinforcements had gone from that neighbourhood to Howe. He wrote at once to Washington, advising him of his peril, and endeavoured to push on; but his delicate frame would stand no more, and on the 15th he went to bed in Mr. Kennedy's house in Peekskill, with so violent an attack of rheumatism that to his bitter disgust he was obliged to resign himself to weeks of inactivity. But he had the satisfaction to receive a letter from Washington approving all that he had done. And in truth he had saved the situation, and Washington never forgot it.

CHAPTER III

Hamilton rejoined the army at Valley Forge and soon recovered his health and spirits. It was well that the spirits revived, for no one else during that terrible winter could lay claim to any. The Headquarters were in a small valley, shut in by high hills white with snow and black with trees that looked like iron. The troops were starving and freezing and dying a mile away, muttering and cursing, but believing in Washington. On a hill beyond the pass Lafayette was comfortable in quarters of his own, but bored and fearing the worst. Laurens chafed at the inaction; he would have had a battle a day. As the winter wore on, the family succumbed to the depressing influence of unrelieved monotony and dread of the future, and only Hamilton knew to what depths of anxiety Washington could descend. But despair had no part in Hamilton's creed. He had perfect faith in the future, and announced it persistently. He assumed the mission of keeping the family in good cheer, and they gave him little time for his studies. As for Washington, even when Hamilton was not at his desk, he made every excuse to demand his presence in the private office; and Hamilton in his prayers humorously thanked his Almighty for the gift of a cheerful disposition. It may be imagined what a relief it was when he and Laurens, Meade, or Tilghman raced each other up the icy gorge to Lafayette's, where they were often jollier the night through than even a cheerful disposition would warrant. Hamilton, although he had not much of a voice, learned one camp-song, "The Drum," and this he sang with such rollicking abandon that it fetched an explosive sigh of relief from the gloomiest breast.

There were other duties from which Hamilton fled to the house on the hill for solace. Valley Forge harboured a heterogeneous collection of foreigners, whose enthusiasm had impelled them to offer swords and influence to the American cause: Steuben, Du Portail, De Noailles, Custine, Fleury, Du Plessis, the three brothers Armand, Ternant, Pulaski, and Kosciusko. They had a thousand wants, a thousand grievances, and as Washington would not be bothered by them, their daily recourse was Hamilton, whom they adored. To him they could lament in voluble French; he knew the exact consolation to administer to each, and when it was advisable he laid their afflictions before Washington or the Congress. They bored him not a little, but he sympathized with them in their Cimmerian exile, and it was necessary to keep them in the country for the sake of the moral effect. But he congratulated himself on his capacity for work.

"I used to wish that a hurricane would come and blow Cruger's store to Hell," he said one day to Laurens, "but I cannot be sufficiently thankful for that experience now. It made me as methodical as a machine, gave my brain a system without which I never could cope with this mass of work. I have this past week dried the tears of seven Frenchmen, persuaded Steuben that he is not Europe, nor yet General Washington, and without too much offending him, written a voluminous letter to Gates calculated to make him feel what a contemptible and traitorous ass he is, yet giving him no chance to run, blubbering, with it to the Congress, and official letters *ad nauseum*. I wish to God I were out of it all, and about to ride into battle at the head of a company of my own."

"And how many widows have you consoled?" asked Laurens. He was huddled in his cot, trying to keep warm.

"None," said Hamilton, with some gloom. "I haven't spoken to a woman for three weeks."

It was a standing joke at Headquarters that Washington always sent Hamilton to console the widows. This he did with such sympathy and tact, such address and energy, that his friends had occasionally been forced to extricate him from complications. But it was an accomplishment in which he excelled as long as he lived.

"The Chief will never let you go," pursued Laurens. "And as there is no one to take your place, you really should not wish it. Washington may be the army, but you are Washington's brain, and of quite as much importance. You should never forget—"

"Come out and coast. That will warm your blood," interrupted Hamilton. His own sense of duty was not to be surpassed, but he had rebellious moods, when preaching suggested fisticuffs.

Outside they met a messenger from Lafayette, begging them to repair to his quarters at once. There they found him entertaining a party of charming women from a neighbouring estate; and a half-hour later the dignity and fashion of Washington's family might have been seen coasting down a steep hill with three Philadelphian exiles, who were as accomplished in many ways as they were satisfying to look upon.

It was one of those days when a swift freeze has come with a rain-storm. Hamilton had stood at the window of the office for an hour, early in the day, biting the end of his quill, and watching the water change to ice as it struck the naked trees, casing every branch until, when the sun came out, the valley was surrounded by a diamond forest, the most radiant and dazzling of winter sights. The sun was still out, its light flashed back from a million facets, the ground was hard and white, the keen cold air awoke the blood, and the three young men forgot their grumblings, and blessed the sex which has alleviated man's burdens so oft and well.

CHAPTER IV

In June the military ardours of this distinguished young trio were gratified to the point of temporary exhaustion. The British evacuated Philadelphia on the 18th, and proceeded up the Delaware in New Jersey. Captain Allan McLane had, as early as May 25th, reported to Washington the enemy's intention to change their quarters for New York, and Washington's desire was to crush them by a decisive blow. At a council of war, however, it was decided merely to hang upon the skirts of the retreating army and avoid an engagement. Lee was aggressive, almost insulting, in counselling inaction, Washington, much embarrassed, but hesitating to ignore the decisions of the council, followed the enemy by a circuitous route, until he reached the neighbourhood of Princeton. The British were in and about Allentown. Washington called another council of war, and urged the propriety of forcing an engagement before the enemy could reach the Heights of Monmouth. Again Lee overruled, being sustained by the less competent generals, who were in the majority. As soon as the council broke up, Hamilton sought out General Greene and led him aside, Greene was white and dejected, but Hamilton's face was hot, and his eyes were flashing.

"I believe that Lee is in the pay of the British or the Conway Cabal," he exclaimed. "I've always believed him ready at any minute to turn traitor. It's a pity he wasn't left to rot in prison. Washington must fight. His honour is at stake. If he lets the British walk off while we sit and whistle, his influence with the army will be gone, Europe will have no more of him, the Conway Cabal will have the excuse it's been watching at keyholes for, and Gates will be Commander-in-chief to-morrow. Will you come with me and persuade him to fight?"

"Yes," said Greene. "And I believe he will. You are like a sudden cold wind on an August day. Come on."

They walked rapidly toward Washington's tent. He was sitting on his camp-stool, but rose as they approached.

"Gentlemen," he said, "I anticipate the object of your visit. You wish me to fight."

"Yes!" exclaimed Hamilton. "As much as you wish it yourself. Why should you regard the councils of the traitorous and the timorous, who, for aught you know, may be in the pay of the Cabal? If the British retreat unmolested, the American army is disgraced. If Congress undertake to manage it, the whole cause will be lost, and the British will be stronger far than when we took up arms—"

"Enough," said Washington. "We fight"

He ordered a detachment of one thousand men, under General Wayne, to join the troops nearest the enemy. Lafayette was given the command of all the advance troops—Lee sulkily retiring in his favour—which amounted to about four thousand. Hamilton was ordered to accompany him and reconnoitre, carry messages between the divisions, and keep Washington informed of the movements of the enemy. There was but a chance that he would be able to fight, but the part assigned to him was not the least dangerous and important at Washington's disposal. The Chief moved forward with the main body of the army to Cranbury.

Clinton had no desire to fight, being encumbered with a train of baggage-wagons and bathorses, which with his troops made a line on the highroad twelve miles long. It being evident that the Americans intended to give battle, he encamped in a strong position near Monmouth Court-house, protected on nearly all sides by woods and marshes. His line extended on the right about a mile and a half beyond the Court-house, and on the left, along the road toward Allentown, for about three miles.

This disposition compelled Washington to increase the advance corps, and he ordered Lee to join Lafayette with two brigades. As senior officer, Lee assumed command of the whole division, under orders to make the first attack. Both Lafayette and Hamilton were annoyed and apprehensive at this arrangement. "Washington is the shrewdest of men in his estimates until it is a matter of personal menace," said Hamilton, "and then he is as trusting as a country wench with a plausible villain. I thought we had delivered him from this scoundrel, and now he has deliberately placed his fortunes in his hands again. Mark you, Lee will serve us some trick before the battle is over."

Hamilton had been galloping back and forth night and day between Lafayette's division and Headquarters, wherever they happened to be, and reconnoitring constantly. The weather was intensely hot, the soil so sandy that his horse often floundered. He had not had a full night's sleep since Washington announced his decision to give battle, and he would have been worn out, had he not been too absorbed and anxious to retain any consciousness of his body. Early on the morning of the 28th, a forward movement being observed on the part of the enemy, Washington immediately put the army in motion and sent word to Lee to press forward and attack.

Lee looked uglier and dirtier than usual, and the very seat of his breeches scowled as he rode forward leisurely. In a few moments he halted, word having been brought him that the main body of the British was advancing.

"If we could but court-martial him on the spot," groaned Lafayette, whose delicate boyish face was crumpled with anxiety.

"He meditates treason!" exclaimed Hamilton. "It is writ all over him."

Having ascertained that the rumour was false, Lee consented to move on again, and the division entered the forest, their advance covered from the British on the plains beyond. For a time Lee manoeuvred so cleverly that Hamilton and Lafayette permitted themselves to hope. Under cover of the forest he formed a portion of his line for action, and with Wayne, Hamilton, and others, rode forward to reconnoitre. Concluding that the column of the British deploying on the right was only a covering party of two thousand, he manoeuvred to cut them off from the main army. Wayne was detached with seven hundred men to attack the covering party in the rear. Lee, with a stronger force, was to gain its front by a road to the left. Small detachments were concealed in the woods. At nine o'clock, the Queen's dragoons being observed upon an eminence near the wood, Lee ordered his light-horse to decoy them to the point where Wayne was posted. The dragoons appeared to fall into the trap, but upon being attacked from the wood, galloped off toward the main column. Wayne started in pursuit; his artillery was raking them, and he had ordered a charge at the point of the bayonet, when, to his amazement, he received an order from Lee to make but a feint of attack and pursuit. He had no choice but to obey, brilliant as might be the victory wrested from him. Lee, meanwhile, dawdled about, although his troops were on one foot with impatience.

Suddenly Sir Henry Clinton, learning that the Americans were marching in force on both his flanks, with the design of capturing his baggage, changed the front of his army by facing about in order to attack Wayne with such deadly fire that the enemy on his flanks would be obliged to fly to the succour of that small detachment. Lafayette immediately saw the opportunity for victory in the rear of the enemy, and rode up to Lee asking permission to make the attempt.

Lee swung his loose head about and scowled at the ardent young Frenchman. "Sir," he replied witheringly, "you do not know British soldiers.

We cannot stand against them. We certainly shall be driven back at first. We must be cautious."

"It may be so, General," replied Lafayette, who would have given much to see that head rolling on the sands; "but British soldiers have been beaten, and they may be again. At any rate, I am disposed to make the trial."

Lee shrugged his shoulders, but as Lafayette sat immovable, his clear hazel eyes interrogating and astonished, he reluctantly gave the Marquis the order to wheel his column to the right and attack the enemy's left. He simultaneously weakened Wayne's detachment and went off to reconnoitre. He afterward claimed that he saw what looked to be the approach of the entire army, and he ordered his right to fall back. The brigades of Scott and Maxwell on the left were already moving forward and approaching the right of the Royal forces, when they received an order from Lee to reënter the wood. At the same time an order was sent to Lafayette to fall back to the Court-house. With a face as flaming as his unpowdered head, he obeyed. Upon reaching the Court-house he learned that a general retreat had begun on the right, under the immediate command of Lee. He had no choice but to follow.

Hamilton, hardly crediting that his worst fears were realized in this unwarranted retreat, galloped over to Lee and urged that possession be taken of a neighbouring hill that commanded the plain on which the enemy were advancing. But Lee protested violently that the Americans had not a chance against that solid phalanx, and Hamilton, now convinced that he meditated the disgrace of the American arms, galloped with all speed in search of Washington.

The retreat, by this, was a panic. The troops fled like an army of terrified rabbits, with that reversion to the simplicity of their dumb ancestors which induces the suspicion that all the manly virtues are artificial. In times of panic man seems to exchange his soul for a tail. These wretches trampled each other into the shifting sand, and crowded many more into the morass. The heat was terrific. They ran with their tongues hanging out, and many dropped dead.

Washington heard of the retreat before Hamilton found him. He was pushing on to Lee's relief when a country-man brought him word of the disgraceful rout. Washington refused to credit the report and spurred forward. Halfway between the meeting-house and the morass he met the head of the first retreating column. He commanded it to halt at once, before the panic be communicated to the main army; then made for Lee. Lee saw him coming and braced himself for the shock. But it was a greater man than Lee who could stand the shock of Washington's temper. He was fearfully roused. The noble gravity of his face had disappeared. It was convulsed with rage.

"Sir," he thundered, "I desire to know what is the reason of this?
Whence arises this confusion and disorder?"

"Sir—" stammered Lee, "sir—" He braced himself, and added impudently: "I thought it best not to beard the enemy in such a situation. It was contrary to my opinion—"

"*Your* opinion!" And then the Chief undammed a torrent of profanity Washingtonian in its grandeur.

He wheeled and galloped to the rallying of the troops. At this moment Hamilton rode up. He had ridden through the engagement without a hat. It seemed to him that he could hear the bubbling of his brain, that the very air blazed, and that the end of all things had come. That day of Monmouth ever remained in his memory as the most awful and hopeless of his life. An ordinary defeat was nothing. But the American arms branded with cowardice, Washington ignobly deposed, inefficient commanders floundering for a few months before the Americans were become the laughing-stock of Europe,—the whole vision was so hideous, and the day so hopeless in the light of those cowardly hordes, that he galloped through the rain of British bullets, praying for death; he had lost all sense of separate existence from the shattered American cause. He did not perceive that Washington had reached the column, and resolved to make one more appeal to Lee, he rode up to that withered culprit and exclaimed passionately:—

"I will stay with you, my dear General, and die with you! Let us all die here, rather than retreat!"

Lee made no reply. His brain felt as if a hot blast had swept it.

"At least send a detachment to the succour of the artillery," said Hamilton, with quick suspicion. And Lee ordered Colonel Livingston to advance.

At the same moment some one told Hamilton that Washington was in the rear, rallying the troops. He spurred his horse and found that the General had rallied the regiments of Ramsay and Stewart, after a rebuke under which they still trembled, and was ordering Oswald to hasten his cannon to the eminence which his aide had suggested to Lee. Hamilton himself was in time to intercept two retreating brigades. He succeeded in rallying them, formed them along a fence at hand, and ordered them to charge at the point of the bayonet. He placed himself at their head, and they made a brilliant dash upon the enemy. But his part was soon over. His horse was shot under him, and as he struck the ground he was overcome by the shock and the heat, and immediately carried from the field. But the retreat was suspended, order restored, and although the battle raged all day, the British gained no advantage. The troops were so demoralized by the torrid heat that at sunset both Commanders were obliged to cease hostilities; and Washington, who had been in the saddle since daybreak, threw himself under a tree to sleep, confident of a victory on the morrow.

"I had a feeling as if my very soul were exploding," said Hamilton to Laurens, as they bathed their heads in a stream in the woods, with the bodies of dead and living huddled on every side of them. "I had a hideous vision of Washington and the rest of us in a huge battle picture, in which a redcoat stood on every squirming variety of continental uniform, while a screeching eagle flew off with the Declaration of Independence. But after all, there is something magnificent in so absolutely identifying yourself with a cause that you go down to its depths of agony and fly to its heights of exaltation. I was mad to die when the day—and with it the whole Cause—seemed lost. Patriotism surely is the master passion. Nothing else can annihilate the ego."

Laurens, who had performed prodigies of valour, sighed heavily. "I felt as you did while the engagement lasted," he replied. "But I went into the battle with exultation, for death this time seemed inevitable. And the only result is a headache. What humiliation!"

"You are morbid, my dear," said Hamilton, tenderly. "You cannot persuade me that at the age of twenty-five naught remains but death—no matter what mistakes one may have made. There is always the public career—for which you are eminently fitted. I would begin life over again twenty times if necessary."

"Yes, because you happen to be a man of genius. I am merely a man of parts. There are many such. Not only is my life ruined, but every day I despair anew of ever attaining that high ideal of character I have set for myself. I want nothing short of perfection," he said passionately. "Could I attain that, I should be content to live, no matter how wretched. But I fall daily. My passions control me, my hatreds, my impulses of the moment. When a man's very soul aches for a purity which it is in man to attain if he will, and when he is daily reminded that he is but a whimperer at the feet of the statue, the world is no place for him."

"Laurens," said Hamilton, warmly, "you refine on the refinements of sensibility. You have brooded until you no longer are normal and capable of logic. Compare your life with that of most men, and hope. You are but twenty-five, and you have won a deathless glory, by a valour and brilliancy on these battlefields that no one else has approached. Your brain and accomplishments are such that the country looks to you as one of its future guides. Your character is that of a Bayard. It is your passions alone, my dear, which save you from being a prig. Passion is the furnace that makes greatness possible. If, when the mental energies are resting, it darts out tongues of flame that strike in the wrong place, I do not believe that the Almighty, who made us, counts them as sins. They are natural outlets, and we should burst without them. If one of those tongues of flame was the cause of your undoing, God knows you have paid in kind. As a rule no one is the worse, while most are better. A certain degree of perfection we can attain, but absolute perfection—go into a wilderness like Mohammed and fast. There is no other way, and even then you merely would have visions; you would not be yourself."

Laurens laughed. "It is not easy to be morbid when you are by. Acquit me for the rest of the night. And it is time we slept. There will be hot work to-morrow. How grandly the Chief rallied! There is a man!"

"He was in a blazing temper," remarked Hamilton. "Lee and Ramsay and Stewart were like to have died of fright. I wish to God he'd strung the first to a gibbet!"

They sought out Washington and lay down beside him. The American army slept as though its soul had withdrawn to another realm where repose is undisturbed. Not so the British army. Sir Henry Clinton did not share Washington's serene confidence in the morrow. He withdrew his weary army in the night, and was miles away when the dawn broke.

Once Washington awoke, raised himself on his elbow, and listened intently. But he could hear nothing but the deep breathing of his weary army. The stars were brilliant. He glanced about his immediate vicinity with a flicker of amusement and pleasure in his eyes. The young men of his household were crowded close about him; he had nearly planted his elbow on Hamilton's profile. Laurens, Tilghman, Meade, even Lafayette, were there, and they barely had left him room to turn over. He knew that these worshipping young enthusiasts were all ready and eager to die for him, and that in spite of his rigid formality they were quite aware of his weak spot, and did not hesitate to manifest their affection. For a moment the loneliest man on earth felt as warmly companioned as if he were raising a family of rollicking boys; then he gently lifted Hamilton out of the way, and slept again. He was bitterly disappointed next morning; but to pursue the enemy in that frightful heat, over a sandy country without water, and with his men but half refreshed, was out of the question.

The rest of the year was uneventful, except for the court-martialling of Lee and his duel with Laurens, who challenged him for his defamation of Washington. Then came the eventful winter of 1779-80, when the army went into quarters at Morristown, Washington and his military family taking possession of a large house belonging to the Widow Ford.

CHAPTER V

"Alexander!" cried a musical but imperious voice.

Hamilton was walking in the depths of the wood, thinking out his financial policy for the immediate relief of the country. He started and faced about. Kitty Livingston sat on her horse, a charming picture in the icy brilliance of the wood. He ran toward her, ripped off her glove, kissed her hand, replaced the glove, then drew back and saluted.

"You are a saucy boy," said Miss Livingston, "and I've a mind to box your ears. I've brought you up very badly; but upon my word, if you were a few years older, I believe I'd marry you and keep you in order, something no other woman will ever be able to do. But I've a piece of news for you—my dear little brother. Betsey Schuyler is here."

Alexander, much to his annoyance, blushed vividly. "And how can you know that I have ever even seen Miss Schuyler?" he asked, rather sulkily.

"*She* told me all about it, my dear. And I inferred from the young lady's manner that she lived but to renew the experience. She is down at Surgeon-General Cochraine's. Mrs. Cochraine is her aunt. Seriously, I want you to be a good little beau, and keep her here as long as possible. She is a great addition to our society; for she is not only one of the belles of the country, accomplished and experienced, but she has an amazing fine character, and I am anxious to know her better. You are still too young to marry, *mon enfant*, but you are so precocious and Miss Schuyler is so charming—if you will marry at your absurd age, you could not do better; for you'll get fine parents as well as a wife, and I've never known a youth more in need of an entire family."

Hamilton laughed. "If I accumulate any more parents," he said, "I shall share the fate of the cat. This morning Colonel Harrison—one of my fathers—almost undressed me to see if my flannels were thick enough, Mrs. Washington gave me a fearful scolding because I went out without a muffler, and even the General is always darting edged glances at the soles of my boots. Yesterday, Laurens, who is two-thirds English, tried to force an umbrella into my hand, but at that I rebelled. If I marry, it will be for the pleasure of taking care of someone else."

He escorted Miss Livingston out to the highroad, and returned to Headquarters, his imagination dancing. He had by no means forgotten Miss Schuyler. That merry roguish high-bred face had shone above many dark horizons, illuminated many bitter winter nights at Valley Forge. He was excited at the prospect of seeing her again, and hastened to arrange a dinner, to which she must be bidden. The young men did as they chose about entertaining, sure of Washington's approval.

"Ah, I know Miss Schuyler well," exclaimed Tilghman, when Hamilton remarked that they should immediately show some attention to the daughter of so illustrious a man as General Schuyler. "I've fetched and carried for her—in fact I once had the honour to be despatched by her mamma to buy her a pair of stays. I fell at her little feet immediately. She has the most lively dark good-natured eyes I ever saw—Good God, Hamilton, are you going to run me through?"

Hamilton for the moment was so convulsed with jealous rage that his very fingers curved, and he controlled them from his friend's throat with an effort. Tilghman's words brought him to his senses, and he laughed heartily. "I was as jealous as Othello, if you'll have the truth, and just why, I vow I don't know, for I met this young lady only once, and that a year ago. I was much attracted, but it's not possible I'm in love with her."

"It's love, my dear boy," said Tilghman, gravely. "Go and ask Steuben if I am not right. Laurens and I will arrange the dinner. You attend to your case immediately."

Hamilton, much concerned, repaired to the house of Baron Steuben. This old courtier and rake was physician in ordinary to all the young men in their numerous cardiacal complications. Hamilton found him in his little study, smoking a huge meerschaum. His weather-beaten face grinned with delight at the appearance of his favourite, but he shook his head solemnly at the revelation.

"I fear this time you are shot, my dear little Hamilton," he said, with much concern. "Have you told me all?"

"All that I can think of." Hamilton was sitting forward on the edge of the chair in considerable dejection. He had not expected this intrication, had hoped the Baron would puff it away.

"Has she a neat waist?"

Hamilton admitted, with some surprise, that her waist was exceptional.

"And her eyes?—I have heard of them—benevolent, yet sparkling;—and a daughter of the Schuylers. Hamilton, believe me, there are worse things than love."

"But I have affairs of the utmost moment on hand at present. I'm revolving a whole financial system, and the correspondence grows heavier every day. I've no time for love."

"My boy," said the former aide to the great Frederick, with emphasis, "when you can work in the sun, why cling to the cold corner of a public hearth? Your brain will spin the faster for the fire underneath. You will write great words and be happy besides. Think of that. What a combination! Mein Gott! You will be terribly in love, my son, but your balance is so extraordinary that your brain will work on just the same. Otherwise I would not dare give such counsel, for without you General Washington would give up, and your poor old Steuben would not have money for tobacco. Give me just one half-sovereign," he added coaxingly.

Hamilton examined the big tobacco pouch and found it two-thirds full. "Not a penny," he said gaily. "The day after to-morrow I will buy you some myself, but I know where that last sovereign went to."

Hamilton took care of the old spendthrift's money, and not only then but as long as he lived. "The Secretary of the Treasury is my banker," said Steuben, years after. "My Hamilton takes care of my money when he cannot take care of his own."

Hamilton retired in some perturbation, and the result of much thinking was that he spent an unconscionable time over his toilet on the evening of the dinner. In his nervousness he tore one of his lace ruffles. Laurens attempted to mend it, and the rent waxed. Hamilton was forced to knock at Mrs. Washington's door and ask her to repair the injury. She was already dressed, in a black lutestring, her hair flat and natural. She looked approvingly at Hamilton, who, not excepting Laurens, was always the most faultlessly dressed member of the family. To-night he wore dark green velvet, fitting closely and exquisitely cut, white silk stockings, and a profusion of delicate lace. His hair was worn in a queue and powdered. It was not till some years later that he conformed to the prevailing fashion and wore a wig.

Mrs. Washington mended the lace, retied the bow of his queue, kissed him and told him to forget the cares of war and correspondence, and enjoy himself. Hamilton retired, much comforted.

It was an imposing family which, a half-hour later, awaited the guests in the drawing-room. Washington was in black velvet and silk stockings, his best white wig spreading in two symmetrical wings. It was a cold grave figure always, and threw an air of solemnity over every scene it loomed upon, which only Hamilton's lively wit could dispel. Laurens wore plum-coloured velvet and much lace, a magnificent court costume. His own figure was no less majestic than Washington's, but his brown eyes and full mouth were almost invariably smiling, despite the canker. He wore a very close wig. Tilghman was in blue, the other men in more sober dress. Lafayette some time since had departed for France, Hamilton having suggested that the introduction of a French military force of six or seven thousand troops would have a powerful effect upon the American army and people.

Lady Sterling arrived with Lady Kitty—the bride of Colonel William Duer since July—her undistinguished homeliness enhancing the smart appearance of her daughter, who was one of the beauties of the time. Lady Kitty had a long oval face, correct haughty little features, and a general air of extreme high breeding. Her powdered hair was in a tower, and she had the tiniest waist and stood upon the highest heels of all the belles. She wore white satin over an immense hoop, a flounce of Spanish lace and a rope of pearls. Kitty Livingston wore yellow which outshone the light of the candles. Susan Boudinot and the other girls were dressed more simply. Mr. Boudinot's eyes were as keen and as kind as ever, his nose seemed longer, and the flesh was accumulating beneath his chin.

The Cochraines and Miss Elizabeth Schuyler were the last to arrive. The northern belle's wardrobe had been an object of much concern to the young ladies now cut off from New York shops, and lamenting the demoralized condition of those in Philadelphia. In Albany all things were still possible. Miss Schuyler wore a pink brocade of the richest and most delicate quality, and a bertha of Brussels lace. The pointed bodice and large paniers made her waist look almost as small as Kitty Duer's, and her feet were the tiniest in the world. She turned them in and walked with a slight shuffle. Hamilton had never seen a motion so adorable. Her hair was rolled out from her face on both sides as well as above, and so thickly powdered that her eyes looked as black as General Washington's coat, while her cheeks and lips were like red wine on pale amber. She blushed as Hamilton bowed before her and offered his arm, and then she felt his heart thump. As for Hamilton, he gave himself up for lost the moment she entered the room, and with the admission, his feelings concentrated with their usual fiery impetuosity. As it was too soon for an outlet, they rushed to his eyes and camped there, to Miss Schuyler's combined discomfort and delight.

For once Hamilton was content to listen, and Miss Schuyler was not loath to entertain this handsome young aide, of whom all the world was talking, and who had haunted her dreams for a year. She had read Milton, Shenstone, and Dodsworth, "The Search after Happiness," by Hannah More, the works of Madame de Genlis, the "Essay on Man," and Shakespeare's lighter plays. Her learning was not oppressive, merely sufficient to give distinction to her mind, and Hamilton was enchanted once more; but he found her most interesting when relating personal anecdotes of encounters with savage warriors in that dark northern land where she had been born and bred, of hideous massacres of which her neighbours had been the victims, of adventurous journeys she had taken with her father, of painted chieftains they had been forced to entertain. She talked with great spirit and no waste of words, and it was evident that she was both sensible and heroic. Hamilton ate little and forgot that he was in a company of twenty people. He was recalled by an abraded shin.

He turned with a jump and encountered Meade's agonized face thrust across Susan Livingston, who sat between them.

"For God's sake, Hamilton, come forth and talk," said Meade, in a hoarse whisper. "There hasn't been a word said above a mutter for three-quarters of an hour. Tilghman gave out long ago. Unless you come to the rescue we'll all be moaning in each other's arms in three minutes."

Hamilton glanced about the table. Washington, looking like himself on a monument, was making not a pretence to entertain poor Lady Sterling, who was almost sniffling. Lord Sterling, having gratified, an hour since, Mrs. Washington's polite interest in his health, was stifling yawn after yawn, and his chubby little visage was oblong and crimson. Tilghman, looking guilty and uncomfortable,—it was his duty to relieve Hamilton at the table,—was flirting with Miss Boudinot. Lady Kitty and Baron Steuben always managed to entertain each other. Laurens and Kitty Livingston were sitting back and staring at each other as they had stared many times before. The others were gazing at their plates or at Hamilton. It was, indeed, a Headquarters dinner at the worst.

It has been remarked that Hamilton had a strong sense of duty. He felt himself unable, even with the most charming girl on the continent beside him, to resist the appeal of all those miserable eyes, and launched forth at once upon the possibilities of Lafayette returning with an army. Everybody responded, and he had many subjects of common interest to discourse brilliantly upon until the long meal finished. Even Washington gave him a grateful glance, and the others reattacked their excellent food with a lost relish, now that the awful silence and sense of personal failure were dispelled by their "bright particular star," as the letters of the day from Morristown and the vicinity cleped our hero. But with Miss Schuyler he had no further word that night, and he retired with the conviction that there were times when there was no satisfaction whatever in doing one's duty.

CHAPTER VI

But a few nights later there was a subscription ball in the commissary storehouse, and Hamilton danced with Miss Schuyler no less than ten times, to the merciless amusement of the family. The ball, the first of any size since the war began, was a fine affair, and had been organized by Tilghman, Meade, and several of the Frenchmen; they were determined upon one gay season, at least. The walls were covered with flags and holly; the women wore their most gorgeous brocades; feathers and jewels were on becoming white wigs or on the towers of powdered hair. All the foreigners were in full regimentals, Steuben, in particular, being half covered with gold lace and orders; the music and supper were admirable. Even Washington looked less careworn than usual, and as he stood apart with Lord Sterling, General Knox, and General Greene, he shed no perceptible chill. Miss Schuyler wore white, with a twist of black velvet in her powdered hair and another about her throat, and would have been the belle of the party had Hamilton permitted other attentions. But she gave him all the dances he demanded, and although her bright manner did not lapse toward sentiment for a moment, he went home so elated that he sat scribbling poetry until Laurens pelted him with pillows and extinguished the candle.

The next day there was a sleighing party to Lord Sterling's, and he drove Miss Schuyler, her aunt, and the wife of General Knox through the white and crystal and blue of a magnificent winter day. Mrs. Cochraine made no secret of her pride in her niece's capture of Washington's celebrated favourite, and assured him of a hearty welcome at her house if he felt disposed to call. He promptly established the habit of calling every evening.

But although he was seriously and passionately in love, and quite sure that Miss Schuyler loved him in return, he hesitated for the first time in his life before precipitating a desired consummation. That he had no money did not worry him in the least, for he knew himself capable of earning any amount, and that the Republic, when free, would bristle with opportunities for young men of parts. But he was in honour bound to tell her of the irregularity of his birth. And in what manner would she regard a possible husband with whose children she never could discuss their father's parents? She was twenty-two, a small woman-of-the-world, not a romantic young miss incapable of reason. And the Schuylers? The proudest family in America! Would they take him on what he had made of himself, on the promise of his future, or would their family pride prove stronger than their common sense? He had moments of frantic doubt and depression, but fortunately there was no time for protracted periods of lover's misery. Washington demanded him constantly for consultation upon the best possible method of putting animation into the Congress and extracting money for the wretched troops. He frequently accompanied the General, as at Valley Forge, in his visits to the encampment on the mountain, where the emaciated tattered wretches were hutting with all possible speed against the severity of another winter. The snow was already on the ground, and every prospect of a repetition of the horrors of Valley Forge. The mere sight of Washington put heart into them, and Hamilton's lively sallies rarely failed to elicit a smile in return.

It so happened that for a fortnight the correspondence with Congress, the States, the Generals, and the British, in regard to the exchange of prisoners, was so heavy, the consultations with Washington so frequent, that Hamilton saw nothing of Miss Schuyler, and had little time for the indulgence of pangs. When he emerged, however, his mind was the freer to seek a solution of the problem which had tormented him, and he quickly found it. He determined to write the truth to Miss Schuyler, and so save the embarrassment he had dreaded for both. To think was to act. He related the facts of his birth and of his ancestry in the briefest possible manner, adding a description of his mother which would leave no question of the place she held in his esteem. He then stated, with the emphasis of which he was master, that he distractedly awaited his dismissal, or Miss Schuyler's permission to declare what he had so awkwardly concealed.

He sent the letter by an orderly, and attacked his correspondence with a desire to put gunpowder on his quill. But Miss Schuyler was a tender-hearted creature and had no intention that he should suffer. She scrawled him a hasty summons to come to her at once, and bade the orderly ride as for his life. Hamilton, hearing a horse coming up the turnpike at runaway pace, glanced out of the window to see what neck was in danger, then flung his quill to the floor and bolted. He was out of the house before the orderly had dismounted, and secured possession of the note. When he had returned to his office, which was in a log extension at the back of the building, he locked the door and read what he could of Miss Schuyler's illegible chirography. That it was a command to wait upon her at once he managed to decipher, but no more at the moment; and feeling as if the heavens had opened, he despatched a hasty note, telling her that he could not leave his work before night, when he would hasten with the pent-up assurances of a love which had been his torment and delight for many weeks. And then he answered a summons to Washington's office, and discussed a letter to the Congress as if there were no such person in the world as Elizabeth Schuyler, as indeed for the hour there was not, nor for the rest of the afternoon.

But at eight o'clock he presented himself at the Cochraine quarters, and Miss Schuyler was alone in the drawing-room. It was some time before they arrived at the question which had weighed so heavily on Hamilton's mind. When, however, they came down to conversation, Miss Schuyler remarked:—

"I am sure that it will make no difference with my dear father, who is the most just and sensible of men. I had never thought of your parentage at all. I should have said you had leapt down from the abode of the gods, for you are much too remarkable to have been merely born. But if he should object—why, we'll run away."

Her eyes danced at the prospect, and Hamilton, who had vowed that nothing should induce him to enter a family where he was not welcome, was by now so hopelessly in love that he was ready to order the chaise and four at once. He remained until Mrs. Cochraine sent him home, then walked up the hill toward Headquarters, keeping to the road by instinct, for he was deep in a reverie on the happiness of the past hours. His dreams were cruelly shattered by the pressure of a bayonet against his breast.

"What?" he demanded. "Oh, the countersign." He racked his memory. It had fled, terrified, from his brain under the rush of that evening's emotions.

"I can't remember it," he said haughtily; "but you know who I am. Let me pass." The sentry stood like a fate.

"This is ridiculous!" cried Hamilton, angrily, then the absurdity of the situation overcame him, and he laughed. Once more he searched his brain for the countersign, which he remembered having given to little Ford just after dinner. Mrs. Ford and her son retained two rooms in the house, and Hamilton frequently gave the youngster the word, that he might play in the village after dark. Suddenly he saw him approaching. He darted down the road, secured the password, and returned in triumph to the sentry.

"Sir," exclaimed the soldier, in dismay, "is this quite regular? Will you give me your word, sir, that it is all right?"

"I vow that no harm shall come to you," said Hamilton. "Shoulder your musket." And there the incident ended, so far as the soldier was concerned, but young Ford carried the story to Headquarters, and it was long before Hamilton heard the last of it.

There was no sleep in him that night. He went to his office and laboured for hours over a verse which should adequately express the love consuming him, and then he awoke Laurens and talked into that sympathetic ear until it was time to break the ice and freshen himself for work.

His work that day was of a vastly different character from the impassioned trifle of the night before. He obtained exemption from other duty, and ordered luncheon and dinner brought to his office. One of the most remarkable examples of Hamilton's mature genius at this age of twenty-three is his long and elaborate letter to Robert Morris on the financial condition of the country, written during the earliest period of his love for Elizabeth Schuyler. As passionate and impatient as he was tender, alive in every part of his nature to the joy of a real affection and to the prospect of a lasting happiness, he yet was able for twelve hours at a time to shut his impending bride in the remotest cupboard of his mind, nor heed her sighs. But there was an older love than Elizabeth Schuyler: a ragged poverty-stricken creature by this, cowering before dangers within and without, raving mad at times, imbecile at others, filling her shattered body with patent nostrums, yet throughout her long course of futilities and absurdities making a desperate attempt to shade the battered lamp of liberty from the fatal draught. Her name was the United States of America, and never was there a more satiric misnomer. If the States chose to obey the requisitions of the Congress, they obeyed them; but as a rule they did not. There was no power in the land to enforce obedience; and they hated each other. As the Congress had demonstrated its inefficiency to the most inactive in public affairs, the contempt of the States is hardly to be wondered at. It is not too much to say that troops were recruited by Washington's influence alone, and kept from mutiny by his immortal magnetism. The finances of the Revolution were in such a desperate condition that Sir Henry Clinton built his hopes of success—now he had discovered that no victory gave him a permanent advantage—upon the dissolution of the American army, possibly an internal war. With depreciated bills in circulation amounting to one hundred and sixty millions of dollars, a public debt of nearly forty millions in foreign and domestic loans, the Congress had, in March, ordered a new emission of bills; the result had been a season of crazy speculation and the expiring gasp of public credit. In addition to an unpaid army, assurances had been given to the French minister that not less than twenty-five thousand men should be ready for the next campaign; and how to force the States to recruit them, and how to pay them when in the field, was the present question between Headquarters and Congress.

From the time that Hamilton's mind had turned to finance, in his nineteenth year, he had devoted the greater part of his leisure to the study and thought of it. Books on the subject were few in those days; the science of political economy was unborn, so far as Hamilton was concerned, for Adam Smith's "Wealth of Nations," published in 1776, had not made its way to America. He assimilated all the data there was to be found, then poured it into the crucible of his creative faculty, and gradually evolved the great scheme of finance which is the locomotive of the United States today. During many long winter evenings he had talked his ideas over with Washington, and it was with the Chief's full approval that he finally went to work on the letter embodying his scheme for the immediate relief of the country. It was addressed to Robert Morris, the Financier of the Revolution.

The first part of the letter was an essay on inflated and depreciated currency, applied personally, the argument based on the three following points: There having been no money in the country, Congress had been unable to avoid the issuance of paper money. The only way to obtain and retire this immense amount of depreciated paper money was to obtain real money. Real money could be obtained in one way only,—by a foreign loan. He then elaborately disposed of the proposed insane methods of applying this projected loan which were agitating the Congress. But he was an architect and builder as well as an iconoclast, and having shown the futility of every financial idea ever conceived by Congress, he proceeded to the remedy. His scheme, then as ever, was a National Bank, to be called The Bank of the United States; the capital to be a foreign loan of two millions sterling.

This letter, even in its details, in the knowledge of human nature it betrays, and in its scheme to combine public and private capital that the wealthy men of the country should, in their own interests, be compelled to support the government, reads like an easy example in arithmetic today; but a hundred and twenty years ago it was so bold and advanced that Morris dared to adopt several of its suggestions in part only, and founded the bank of Pennsylvania on the greater plan, by way of experiment. No one but Hamilton could carry out his own theories.

Hamilton, who often had odd little attacks of modesty, signed the letter, James Montague; address, Morristown. He read it to Washington before posting.

The Chief, whose men were aching, sighed heavily.

"They will pick a few crumbs out of it," he said. "But they will not make a law of it in toto; the millennium is not yet come. But if it gives them one idea we should be thankful, it being a long and weary time since they have experienced that phenomenon. If it does not, I doubt if these men fight another battle. I wonder if posterity will ever realize the indifference of their three million ancestors to the war which gave them their independence—if we accomplish that end. I ask for soldiers and am treated much as if I had asked for my neighbour's wife. I ask for money to keep them from starving and freezing and am made to feel like an importunate beggar."

"I had a letter from Hugh Knox not so long since," said Hamilton, in his lightest tone; for Washington was on the verge of one of his attacks of infuriated depression, which were picturesque but wearing. "He undertakes to play the prophet, and he is an uncommon clever man, sir: he says that you were created for the express purpose of delivering America, to do it single-handed, if necessary, and that my proud destiny is to be your biographer. The first I indorse, so does every thinking man in the country. But for the second—alas! I am not equal to a post of such exalted honour."

Washington smiled. "No one knows better than your old Chief that your destiny is no such ha'penny affair as that. But at least you wouldn't make an ass of me. God knows what is in store for me at the hands of scribblers."

"You lend yourself fatally well to marble and stone, sir," said Hamilton, mischievously. "I fear your biographers will conceive themselves writing at the feet of a New World Sphinx, and that its frozen granite loneliness will petrify their image of you."

"I like the prospect! I am unhappily conscious of my power to chill an assemblage, but the cold formality of my manner is a safeguard, as you know. My nature is one of extremes; if I did not encase myself, I should be ramming every man's absurd opinions down his throat, and letting my cursed temper fly at each of the provocations which constantly beset me. I have not the happy gift of compromise; but I am not unhuman, and I like not the prospect of going down to posterity a wooden figurehead upon some emblematic battle-ship. Perhaps, my boy, you, who best know me, will be moved by charity to be my biographer, after all."

"I'll make it the business of my old age, sir; I pledge you my word, and no one loves you better nor can do you such justice as I. When my work in the National Family is done, then shall I retire with my literary love, an old and pleasant love; and what higher subject for my pen?"

He spoke in a tone of badinage, for he was bent on screwing up Washington's spirits, but he made his promise in good faith, nevertheless, and Washington looked at him with deep affection.

"My mind is certainly easier," he said, in a tone that was almost light.
"Go now and post your letter, and give your evening to

Miss Schuyler.

Present my compliments to her."

"I became engaged to her last night, sir."

"Ah! had you forgotten to tell me?"

"No, sir; I have but just remembered it."

Washington laughed heartily. "Mind you never tell her that," he said. "Women love the lie that saves their pride, but never an unflattering truth. You have learned your lesson young,—to put a tempting face aside when duty demands every faculty; it is a lesson which takes most men longest to learn. I could tell you some amusing stories of rough and tumbles in my mind between the divine image of the hour and some affair of highest moment. But to a brain like yours all things are possible."

He rose, and took Hamilton's hand and shook it warmly.

"God bless you," he said. "Your future unrolls to my vision, brilliant and happy. I deeply wish that it may be so."

CHAPTER VII

The letter from General Schuyler, giving his consent to the engagement, has not been preserved; but some time after he had occasion to write Hamilton a business letter, in which the following passage occurs:—

> You cannot, my dear sir, be more happy at the connexion you have made with my family than I am. Until the child of a parent has made a judicious choice, his heart is in continual anxiety; but this anxiety was removed on the moment I discovered it was on you she had placed her affections. I am pleased with every instance of delicacy in those who are so dear to me; and I think I read your soul on the occasion you mention. I shall therefore only entreat you to consider me as one who wishes in every way to promote your happiness.

General Schuyler was ordered by Congress to Morristown to confer with Washington. He took a house, sent for his family, and remained until late in the summer. The closest friendship was formed between Schuyler and Hamilton, which, with common political interests and deepening sympathy, increased from year to year. The good fairies of Nevis who had attended Hamilton's birth never did better for him than when they gave him Elizabeth Schuyler for wife and Philip Schuyler for father and friend. And they had blasted the very roots of the chief impediment to success, for he triumphed steadily and without effort over what has poisoned the lives of many men; and triumphed in spite of the fact that the truth was vaguely known always, and kept in the quiver of his enemies.

As Hamilton was absent from Headquarters but seldom during General Schuyler's sojourn, the lovers met almost every evening, and occasionally Washington, who possessed certain sympathies based on long experience, would give Hamilton a morning free, and suggest a ride through the woods. Never were two people happier nor more inherently suited. Hamilton's instinct had guided him safely past more brilliant women to one who willingly would fold herself round his energetic individuality of many parts, fitting into every division and crevice. She was receptive, sympathetic, adaptive, with sufficient intelligence to appreciate the superlative brain of the man whom she never ceased to worship and to regard as a being of unmortal clay. A brilliant ambitious wife in the same house with Hamilton might have written a picturesque diary, but the domestic instrument would have twanged with discords. Hamilton was unselfish, and could not do enough for those he loved; but he was used to the first place, to the unquestioned yielding of it to his young high-mightiness by his clever aspiring friends, by the army of his common acquaintance, and in many ways by Washington himself. Had he married Angelica Schuyler, that independent, high-spirited, lively, adorable woman, probably they would have boxed each other's ears at the end of a week.

Hamilton made the dash on Staten Island with Lord Sterling, and in March went with General St. Clair and Colonel Carrington to negotiate with the British commissioners for the exchange of prisoners; before the battle of Springfield he was sent out to reconnoitre. Otherwise his days were taken up bombarding the Congress with letters representing the necessity of drafting troops to meet the coming emergencies.

He and Miss Betsey Schuyler had a very pretty plan, which was nothing less than that they should go to Europe on their wedding tour, Congress to find his presence necessary at the Court of France. The suggestion originated with Laurens, who had been asked to go as secretary to Franklin. He had no wish to go, and knowing Hamilton's ardent desire to visit Europe and growing impatience with his work, had recommended his name to the Congress. General Schuyler would have procured a leave of absence for his impending son-in-law, and sent the young couple to Europe with his blessing and a heavy wallet, but Hamilton would as soon have forged a man's name as travelled at his expense. He hoped that the Congress would send him. He was keenly alive to the value of studying Europe at first hand before he was called upon to help in the modelling of the new Republic, and the vision of wandering in historic lands with his bride kept him awake at night. Moreover, he was desperately tired of his life at Headquarters. When the expedition to Staten Island was in question, he asked Washington, through Lafayette, to give him the command of a battalion which happened to be without a field-officer. Washington refused, partly from those motives of policy to which he ever showed an almost niggling adherence, but more because he could not spare his most useful aide. Hamilton, who was bursting for action of any sort, retired to his detested little office in angry disappointment. But he was a philosopher. He adjusted himself to the Inevitable, and dismissed the matter from his mind, after registering a vow that he would take advantage of the first excuse which might offer to resign his position.

The Schuylers returned to Albany. The French fleet arrived, and hovered well beyond the range of British guns, having no desire to risk an engagement until reinforced. Its Admiral, Count Rochambeau, having a grievance, Hamilton advised a personal conference.

"We might suggest that he meet us halfway—say at Wethersfield, near Hartford," he added. "That would save us something in travelling expenses."

> Washington sighed heavily. "We are worse off than you
> think," he said.
> "I might scrape together money enough for half the
> journey, but no more.
> Lafayette and his aide must go with us—to say nothing
> of the escort.
> Think of the innkeepers' bills, for ourselves and horses.
> What to do I confess I do not know, for I should confer
> with this Frenchman at once."

"Go we must, sir," said Hamilton, decidedly, "if we have to take up a collection—why not? If an object cannot be accomplished one way, try another." He stood up and emptied the contents of his pockets on the table. "Only five hundred beggarly continentals," he said ruefully. "However, who knows what treasures may line more careful pockets than mine? I know they will come forth as spontaneously. Have I your permission to try, sir?"

Washington nodded, and Hamilton ran downstairs, pressed Meade into service, and together they made the round of the officers' quarters. He returned at the end of an hour and threw a huge bundle of paper on the table. "Only eight thousand dollars, sir," he said. "It's the best that any man could do. But I think it may carry us through."

"It will have to," said Washington. "Remind me, my dear boy, if you see me eating too much. I have such an appetite!"

They set out on their journey a week later, having communicated with Rochambeau, who agreed to meet them at Wethersfield. All went well, for the wretched inns were not exorbitant, until they reached Hartford. They arrived late in the afternoon, weary and ravenous. After a bath and a glimpse of luxurious beds, they marched to the dining room and sat down to a sumptuous repast, whose like had greeted neither nostril nor palate for many a day. The wines were mellow, the tobacco green, the conversation gay until midnight. Hamilton sang "The Drum," and many another song rang among the rafters. Washington retired first, bidding the youngsters enjoy themselves. The young men arose at their accustomed hour next morning, with appetites renewed, but waited in vain for their Chief. Hamilton finally knocked at his door. There was no response, and a servant told him that the General had gone out nearly an hour before. He went in search, bidding Lafayette and M'Henry remain behind. As he had anticipated, he found Washington in a secluded nook, engaged in prayer. He waited a few moments, then coughed respectfully. Washington immediately rose, his harassed face showing little relief.

"Is anything wrong, sir?" asked Hamilton, anxiously.

"Alas!" said the General, "I wonder that you, too, are not driven to prayer, to intercede for help in this distressing predicament. Think of that extravagant repast we consumed last night. God help me, but I was so famished I never gave a thought to consequences. Unquestionably, the breakfast will be on a like scale. *And we have but eight thousand dollars with which to pay the bill!*"

"It is true! I never gave the matter a thought—I am cursedly extravagant. And we must get home! I suppose we shall have to fast all the way. Well, we've fasted before, and the memory of last night's dinner may sustain us—"

"But this man's bill! How are we to meet it?"

"Shall I speak to him, sir? Tell him unreservedly our predicament—that these wretched eight thousand dollars are all we have in the world? Perhaps he is a good patriot, and will call the account square."

"Do," said Washington, "and come here and tell me what he says. I am too mortified to show my face. I shall not enter the house again."

Hamilton walked slowly to the house, little caring for his errand. He returned on a dead run.

"We are saved, sir!" he cried, almost in Washington's arms. "Governor Trumbull has sent word to all the hostelries that we are to be his guests while we are in the state of Connecticut!"

Washington said his prayers again, and ate two chickens for breakfast.

On the return from this conference, when approaching the house of General Benedict Arnold, opposite West Point, where they were invited for breakfast, Washington suddenly decided to accompany Lafayette, who wished to inspect some earthworks.

"You need not come," he said to Hamilton and M'Henry. "I know that you are both in love with Mrs. Arnold. Go on. We will join you presently."

The young men were greeted with effusion by the pretty hostess, with absent reserve by her husband. Mrs. Arnold left the room to order that the breakfast be delayed. While she was absent, a note was brought to Arnold. He opened it, turned green, and rising hastily, announced that his presence was demanded at West Point and left the room. The sound of a smothered scream and fall came from above. A moment later the aides heard the sound of galloping hoofs.

Their suspicions aroused, they ran outside. A messenger, with a despatch from Colonel Jameson, awaited Washington's arrival. Hamilton tore open the paper. It contained the news that a British spy had been captured within the lines. In an instant Hamilton and M'Henry were on their horses and off in pursuit of the fugitive. That Arnold was a traitor and had fled to the British war-ship, *Vulture,* hovering in Haverstraw Bay, a slower wit than Hamilton's would have assumed. The terrified scoundrel was too quick for them. He had ridden over a precipice to the shore below, and under protection of a flag of truce was far down the river when his pursuers sighted him. They returned with all speed.

I shall not repeat the oft-told tale of André's capture, trial, and death. Nowhere has it been so well told as by Hamilton himself, in a letter to Laurens, printed at the time and universally read. It is only necessary here to allude to his share in that unhappiest episode of the war. When Washington reached the house his aide was engaged in consoling Mrs. Arnold, who was shrieking and raving, weeping and fainting; imposing on Hamilton a task varied and puzzling, even to one of his schooling. But she was very young, very charming, and in a tragic plight. Washington himself wiped away a tear, and for a moment forgot the barely averted consequences of her husband's treason, while he assisted Hamilton in assuaging a grief so bitter and so appealing. As soon as was possible he sent her through the British lines.

But Hamilton quickly forgot Mrs. Arnold in his sympathy and admiration for the unfortunate André. He conceived a quick and poignant friendship for the brilliant accomplished young Englishman, with the dreamy soft face of a girl, and a mettle which had brought him to destruction. Hamilton did all he could to save him, short of suggesting to André to ask Sir Henry Clinton to offer Arnold in exchange. He enlisted the sympathy of the officers at West Point in the prisoner's behalf, gave up his leisure to diverting André's mind, and persuaded Washington to delay the execution and send an indirect suggestion to Clinton to offer the exchange himself. When all hope was over, he personally begged Washington to heed André's request for a soldier's death, and not condemn such a man to the gibbet. Washington gladly would have saved his interesting prisoner's life, and felt deeply for him, but again those motives of policy prevailed, and André was executed like a common malefactor.

CHAPTER VIII

Washington was in temporary quarters—a cramped and wretched tavern—at Liberty Pole, New Jersey. The inaction being oppressive, Hamilton concentrated his thoughts on the condition and needs of the country.

> I am sorry that the same spirit of indifference to public affairs prevails, [he wrote to Sears]. It is necessary we should rouse and begin to do our business in earnest, or we shall play a losing game. We must have a government with more power. We must have a tax in kind. We must have a foreign loan. We must have a bank on the true principles of a bank. We must have an administration distinct from Congress, and in the hands of single men under their orders. We must, above all things, have an army for the war.... We are told here there is to be a Congress of the neutral powers at the Hague for meditating of peace. God send it may be true. We want it; but if the idea goes abroad, ten to one if we do not fancy the thing done, and fall into a profound sleep till the cannon of the enemy waken us next campaign. This is our national character.

Hamilton, the High Priest of Energy, had long since declared war against the genius of the American people, who believed in God and the art of leisure. Hamilton believed in God and a cabinet of zealous ministers. He was already a thorn in the side of estimable but hesitant patriots, and in times to come his unremitting and remorseless energy was to be a subject of reproach by associates and enemies alike. Even Jefferson, that idol of the present as of the past democracy, had timidly declared against separation in 1774, while Hamilton, a boy of seventeen, had been the first to suggest the resort to arms, and incessant in his endeavours until the great result was accomplished. He had countless other schemes, and he knew that eventually he would succeed in driving the American people before the point of his quill. That his task would be long and arduous did not daunt him for a moment. By this time he knew every want of the country, and was determined upon the reorganization of the government. The energy which is one of the distinguishing characteristics of the American nation to-day was generated by Hamilton, might, indeed, be said to be the persistence and diffusion of his ego. For the matter of that, all that is greatest in this American evolution of a century was typified in Hamilton. Not only his formidable energy, but his unqualified honour and integrity, his unquenchable optimism, his extraordinary nimbleness of mind and readiness of resource, his gay good-nature, high spirits, and buoyancy, his light philosophy effervescing above unsounded depths, his inability to see when he was beaten, his remorseless industry, his hard common sense, combined with a versatile cleverness which makes for shallowness in another race, his careless generosity, his aptitude for detail and impatience of it, his reckless bravery in war and intrepidity in peace, even his highly strung nerves, excitability, and obliging readiness at all times for a fight, raise him high above history as the genius of the American race. The reverse side of the national character we owe to the greatest of his rivals; as will be seen hereafter.

During the sojourn at Liberty Pole, Washington and he sat through many nights discussing the imperative need of the reorganization of the government, and the best methods by which it could be accomplished. The result was Hamilton's letter to James Duane, an important member of the Congress.

This letter, no doubt the most remarkable of its kind ever written, and as interesting to-day as when Hamilton conceived it, is far too long to be quoted. It began with an exhaustive analysis of the reasons for the failure of Congress to cope with a situation which was becoming more threatening every hour, and urged the example of the Grecian republics and the Swiss cantons against the attempted confederation of the States without a strong centralized government. Lacking a common tie of sufficient strength, the States would inevitably drift toward independent sovereignty, and they had given signal proof in the matter of raising troops, contributing money, and in their everlasting disputes about boundary lines, as to the absolute lack of any common public spirit. His remedy, in brief, was a convention of the States for the purpose of creating a Federal Constitution, the distributing of the powers of government into separate departments, with Presidents of War, Marine, and Trade, a secretary of Foreign Affairs, and a Financier, defining their prerogatives; the States to have no privileges beyond an internal police for the protection of the property and the rights of individuals, and to raise money by internal taxes; the army to be recruited on a permanent establishment. In addition, there was an elaborate system of taxation, by which the country could be supported in all its emergencies. His favourite plan of a National Bank was elaborated in minute detail, the immediate necessity for a foreign loan dwelt upon with sharp reproof, and examples given of the recruiting of armies in European states.

Out of a multitude of suggestions a few were adopted within a short time, but the great central suggestion, the calling of a convention for the purpose of creating a Federal Constitution, was to be hammered at for many weary years before jealous States and unconfident patriots could be persuaded to a measure so monarchical and so bold. But the letter is on record, and nothing more logical, far-sighted, and comprehensive ever was written. It contained the foundation-stones upon which this government of the United States stands to-day. Congress put on its spectacles and read it with many grunts, magnanimously expressing admiration for a youth who had fearlessly grappled with questions which addled older brains; but its audacious suggestions of a government greater than Congress, and of a bank which would add to their troubles, were not taken seriously for a moment.

Hamilton also found time to write a good many love letters. Here is one of them:—

> I would not have you imagine, Miss, that I write you so often to gratify your wishes or please your vanity; but merely to indulge myself, and to comply with that restless propensity of my mind which will not be happy unless I am doing something in which you are concerned. This may seem a very idle disposition in a philosopher and a soldier, but I can plead illustrious examples in my justification. Achilles liked to have sacrificed Greece and his glory to a female captive, and Anthony lost a world for a woman. I am very sorry times are so changed as to oblige me to go to antiquity for my apology, but I confess, to the disgrace of the present time, that I have not been able to find as many who are as far gone as myself in the laudable Zeal of the fair sex. I suspect, however, if others knew the charm of my sweetheart as I do, I could have a great number of competitors. I wish I could give you an idea of her. You can have no conception of how sweet a girl she is. It is only in my heart that her image is truly drawn. She has a lovely form and still more lovely mind. She is all goodness, the gentlest, the dearest, the tenderest of her sex. Ah, Betsey, how I love her!

His reiterated demand for a foreign loan, and the sending of a special envoy to obtain it, at last wrung a reluctant consent from Congress. Lafayette was his politic suggestion, and Congress would have indorsed it, but that adventurous young hero had not come to America to return and beg money on his own doorstep. There was a prospect of fighting in the immediate future, and he was determined to add to his renown. The choice then lay between Hamilton and Laurens, who had received the thanks of Congress for his distinguished services in the field, and whose father had been a president of that body. Lafayette and all the Frenchmen were anxious that the mission be given to Hamilton. The former went to Philadelphia and talked to half the Congress. He offered Hamilton private letters which would introduce him to the best society of Europe; adding, "I intend giving you the *key* of the cabinet, as well as of the societies which influence them."

Laurens, by this time, was eager to go. His father, who had started for Holland as Minister Plenipotentiary, had been captured by the British and confined in the Tower of London; the foreign mission would give him an opportunity to attempt his liberation. Moreover, life was very dull at present, and he knew himself to be possessed of diplomatic talents. But he was also aware of Hamilton's ardent desire to visit Europe, all that it would mean to that insatiate mind, his weariness of his present position. Washington would give his consent to the temporary absence of Hamilton, for the French money was the vital necessity of the Republic's life, and he knew that his indomitable aide would not return without it Therefore Laurens wrote to Hamilton, who was in Albany awaiting his wedding-day, that he should resign in his favour, and congratulated him on so brilliant and distinguished a honeymoon.

The struggle in Hamilton's mind was brief. The prospect of sailing with his bride on a long and delightful journey that could not fail to bring him highest honour had made his blood dance. Moreover, in the previous month Washington had again refused his request for an independent command. It took him but a short time to relinquish this cherished dream when he thought of the unhappy plight of Mr. Laurens, and remembered the deep anxiety of the son, often expressed. He wrote to Laurens, withdrawing in the most decisive terms. Laurens was not to be outdone. He loved his father, but he loved Hamilton more. He pressed the appointment upon his friend, protesting that the affairs of the elder Laurens would be quite as safe in his hands. Hamilton prevailed, and Congress, having waited amiably while the two martial youths had it out, unanimously appointed Laurens. He could not sail until February, and as soon as the matter was decided obtained leave of absence and repaired in all haste to Albany, to be present at Hamilton's wedding.

CHAPTER IX

The wedding of Alexander Hamilton and Elizabeth Schuyler was the most notable private event of the Revolution. The immense social and political consequence of the Schuylers, and the romantic fame of the young aide, of whom the greatest things possible were expected, brought the aristocracy of New York and the Jersies to Albany despite the inclement winter weather. The large house of the Schuylers gave a prolonged hospitality to the women, and the men lodged in the patriarchal little town. But although Hamilton was glad to see the Livingstons, Sterlings, and Boudinots again, the greater number of the guests interested him far less than a small group of weather-beaten soldiers, of which this occasion was the happy cause of reunion. Troup was there, full of youth and honours. He had received the thanks of Congress for his services at Saratoga, and been appointed secretary of the Board of War. Recently he had resigned from the army, and was completing his law studies. Nicolas Fish came with Lafayette, whose light artillery he commanded. He was known as a brave and gallant soldier, and so excellent a disciplinarian that he had won the approval and confidence of Washington. He still parted his little fringe in the middle, and his face was as chubby as ever, his eyes as solemn. Lafayette, who had brought a box full of clothes that had dazzled Paris, embraced Hamilton with tears, but they were soon deep in conjectures of the next campaign. Laurens, looking like a king in exile, wrung many hearts. Hamilton's brother aides, unfortunately, were the more closely bound by his absence, but they had despatched him with their blessing and much chaffing.

The hall of the Schuyler mansion was about twenty feet square and panelled in white. It was decorated with holly, and for three nights before the wedding illuminated by hundreds of wax candles, while the young people danced till three in the morning. The Schuyler house, long accustomed to entertaining, had never been gayer, and no one was more content than the chatelaine. Although she had been reasonably sure of Elizabeth, there was no telling at what moment the maiden might yield to the romantic mania of the time, and climb out of her window at night while Hamilton stood shivering below. Now all danger was past, and Mrs. Schuyler moved, large, placid, and still handsome, among her guests, beaming so affectionately whenever she met Mrs. Carter's flashing eyes that Peggy and Cornelia renewed their vows to elope when the hour and the men arrived. General Schuyler, once more on the crest of public approval, was always grave and stern, but he, too, breathed satisfaction and relief. He was a tall man of military appearance, powerful, muscular, slender; but as his nose was large and fleshy, and he wore a ragged-looking wig with wings like Washington's, he could not be called handsome. It was a noble countenance, however, and his black eyes flashed and pierced.

As for Hamilton and Miss Schuyler, who had a trunk full of charming new gowns, they were as happy as two children, and danced the night through. They were married on the 20th, in the drawing-room, in front of the splendid mantel, which the housewives had spent much time in admiring. The bride wore the white which became her best, made with a long pointed bodice and paniers, and lace that had been worn by the wife of the first patroon. She had risen to the dignity of a wig, and her mass of black hair was twisted mercilessly tight under the spreading white monstrosity to which her veil was attached. Hamilton wore a black velvet coat, as befitting his impending state. Its lining and the short trousers were of white satin. His shapely legs were in white silk, his feet in pumps with diamond buckles, the present of Lafayette. He, too, wore a wig,—a close one, with a queue,—but he got rid of it immediately after the ceremony, for it heated his head.

Hamilton had then reached his full height, about five feet six. His bride was perhaps three inches shorter. The world vowed that never had there been so pretty a couple, nor one so well matched in every way. Both were the perfection of make, and the one as fair and fresh as a Scot, the other a golden gipsy, the one all fire and energy, the other docile and tender, but with sufficient spirit and intelligence. It is seldom that the world so generously gives its blessing, but it might have withheld it, for all that Hamilton and his bride would have cared.

Hamilton's honeymoon was brief. There was a mass of correspondence awaiting him, and no place for a bride in the humble Dutch house at New Windsor where Washington had gone into winter quarters. But the distance was not great, and he could hope for flying leaves of absence. Washington was not unsympathetic to lovers; he had been known to unbend and advise his aides when complications threatened or a siege seemed hopeless; and he had given Hamilton the longest leave possible. Nevertheless, the bridegroom set forth, one harsh January morning, on his long journey, over roads a foot deep in snow, and through solitary winter forests, with any thing but an impassioned desire to see General Washington again. Had he been returning to the command of a corps, with a prospect of stirring events as soon as the snow melted, he would have spurred his horse with high satisfaction, even though he left a bride behind him; but to return to a drudgery which he hated the more for having escaped it for three enchanted weeks, made his spirit turn its back to the horse's head. He resolved anew to resign if an opportunity offered. Four years of that particular sort of devotion to the patriot cause were enough. He wished to demonstrate his patriotism in other ways. He had accomplished the primary object for which Washington had pressed him into service, and he believed that the war was nearing its finish; there was nothing he could now do at Headquarters which the other aides could not do as well, and he wanted military excitement and renown while their possibilities existed.

CHAPTER X

The first task awaiting him upon his arrival at Headquarters was to draw up a letter of instruction for Laurens, a task which required minute care; for on its suggestions, as much as on Laurens's brilliant talents, depended the strength of a mission whose failure might mean that of the American arms. Laurens had requested the letter, and told Hamilton that he should be guided by it. He did not anticipate a royal condition of mind which would prompt him practically to carry off the French money-bags under the king's astonished nose, and he knew Hamilton's command of every argument connected with the painful subject of financial needs. Hamilton drew up a lucid and comprehensive letter, in nine parts, which Laurens could study at his leisure on the frigate, *Alliance*; then attacked his accumulated duties. They left him little leisure to remember he was a bridegroom, although he occasionally directed his gaze toward the North with some longing. His freedom approached, however, and it was swift and unexpected.

It came on the 16th of February. His office was in his bedroom. He had just completed a letter containing instructions of an important nature for the commissary, and started in search of Tilghman, whose duty it was to see it safely delivered. On the stairs he passed Washington, whose brow was heavy. The General, with that brevity which was an indication of his passionate temper fighting against a self-control which he must have knocked flat with great satisfaction at times, ejaculated that he wished to speak with him at once. Hamilton replied that he would wait upon him immediately, and hastened to Tilghman's office, wondering what had occurred to stir the depths of his Chief. He was but a moment with Tilghman, but on the stairs he met Lafayette, who was in search of him upon a matter of business. It is possible that Hamilton should not have permitted himself to be detained, but at all events he did, for perhaps two minutes. Suddenly he became conscious that Washington was standing at the head of the stairs, and wondering if he had awaited him there, he abruptly broke off his conversation with Lafayette, and ran upward. Washington looked as if about to thunder anathema upon the human race. He had been annoyed since dawn, and his passions fairly flew at this last indignity.

"Colonel Hamilton!" he exclaimed. "You have kept me waiting at the head of the stairs these ten minutes. I must tell you, sir, you treat me with disrespect."

Hamilton's eyes blazed and his head went back, but his quick brain leapt to the long-desired opportunity. He replied as calmly as if his heart were not thumping, "I am not conscious of it, sir, but since you have thought it necessary to tell me so, we part."

"Very well, sir!" replied Washington, "if it be your choice!" He turned his back and strode to his office.

Hamilton went to his room with a light heart, feeling as if the pigeon-holes were marching out of his brain. The breach was Washington's; he himself had answered with dignity, and could leave with a clear conscience. He had not kept Washington waiting above four minutes, and he did not feel that an apology was necessary.

"Oh," he thought aloud, "I feel as if I had grown wings." He would return to his bride for a few weeks, then apply once more for a command.

There was a knock, and Tilghman entered. The young men looked at each other in silence for a moment; Tilghman with an almost comical anxiety, Hamilton with alert defiance.

"Well?" demanded Hamilton.

"I come from the Chief—ambassador extraordinary. Look out of the window, or I shall not have courage to go on. He's put the devil to bed and is monstrous sorry this misunderstanding has occurred—"

"Misunderstanding?" snorted Hamilton.

"You know my love of euphony, Hamilton. Pray let me finish. I'd rather be Laurens on my way to beg. What is a king to a lion? But seriously, my dear, the Chief is desperately sorry this has occurred. He has deputed me to assure you of his great confidence in your abilities, integrity, and usefulness, and of his desire, in a candid conversation, to heal a difference which could not have happened but in a moment of passion. Do go and see him at once, and then we shall all sleep in peace to-night."

But Hamilton shook his head decidedly. "You know how tired I am of all this," he said, "and that I can be as useful and far more agreeably active in the field. If I consent to this interview, I am lost. I have never doubted the Chief's affection for me, but he is also the most astute of men, and knows my weakness. If, arguments having failed, he puts his arm about my shoulders and says, 'My boy, *do* not desert me,' I shall melt, and vow that neither bride nor glory could beckon me from him. So listen attentively, mon ami, and deliver my answer as follows: 1st. I have taken my resolve in a manner not to be revoked, 2d. As a conversation could serve no other purpose than to produce explanations, mutually disagreeable, though I certainly will not refuse an interview if he desires it, yet I should be happy if he would permit me to decline it. 3d. That, though determined to leave the family, the same principles which have kept me so long in it will continue to direct my conduct toward him when out of it. 4th. That I do not wish to distress him or the public business by quitting him before he can derive other assistance by the return of some of the gentlemen who are absent. 5th. And that in the meantime it depends on him to let our behaviour to each other be the same as if nothing had happened."

Tilghman heaved a deep sigh. "Then you really mean to go?" he said. "Heartless wretch! Have you no mercy on us? Headquarters will be a tomb, with Washington reposing on top. Think of the long and solemn breakfasts, the funereal dinners, the brief but awful suppers. Washington will never open his mouth again, and I never had the courage to speak first. If ever you deign to visit us, you will find that we have lost the power of speech. I repeat that you have no heart in your body."

Hamilton laughed. "If you did not know that I love you, you would not sit there and revile me. No family has ever been happier than ours. In four years there has not been a quarrel until to-day. I can assure you that my heart will ache when the time comes to leave you, but I really had got to the end of my tether. I have long felt as if I could not go on another day."

"'Tis grinding, monotonous work," admitted Tilghman, "and we've all wondered how you have stood it as long as this—every bit of you was made for action. Well, I'll take your message to the Chief."

Washington consented to waive the explanation and sent Hamilton another message, thanking him for consenting to remain until Harrison and Meade returned.

CHAPTER XI

Little Mrs. Hamilton was delighted with the course affairs had taken, and pleaded for resignation from the army. But to this Hamilton would not hearken. Anxious as he was for the war to finish, that he might begin upon the foundations of home and fortune, he had no intention of deserting a cause to which he had pledged himself, and in which there still was a chance for him to achieve distinction. So far, his ambitions were wholly military. If the profound thought he had given to the present and future needs of the Republic was not wholly impersonal; if he took for granted that he had a part to play when the Revolution finished, it was little more than a dream at present. His very temperament was martial, the energy and impetuosity of his nature were in their element on the battlefield, and he would rather have been a great general than the elder Pitt. But although there is no reason to doubt that he would have become a great general, had circumstance favoured his pet ambition, yet Washington was a better judge of the usefulness of his several abilities than he was himself. Not only had that reader of men made up his mind that a brain like his favourite's should not be wasted on the battlefield,—left there, perhaps, while dolts escaped, for Hamilton had no appreciation of fear or danger,—but he saw in him the future statesman, fertile, creative, executive, commanding; and he could have no better training than at a desk in his office. Phenomenally precocious, even mature, as Hamilton's brain had been when they met that morning on the Heights of Harlem, these four years had given it a structural growth which it would not have acquired in camp life, and to which few men of forty were entitled. Of this fact Hamilton was appreciative, and he was too philosophical to harbour regrets; but that period was over now, and he wanted to fight.

On April 27th he wrote to Washington, asking for employment during the approaching campaign, suggesting the command of a light corps, and modestly but decidedly stating his claims.

Washington was greatly embarrassed. Every arbitrary appointment caused a ferment in the army, where jealousies were hotter than martial ardours. Washington was politic above all things, but to refuse Hamilton a request after their quarrel and parting was the last thing he wished to do. He felt that he had no choice, however, and wrote at once, elaborating his reasons for refusal, ending as follows:—

> My principal concern rises from an apprehension that you will impute my refusal of your request to other motives than those I have expressed, but I beg you to be assured I am only influenced by the reasons I have mentioned.

Hamilton knew him too well to misunderstand him, but he was deeply disappointed. He retired into the library behind the drawing-room of the Schuyler mansion, and wrote another and a more elaborate letter to Robert Morris. He began with a reiteration of the impotence of Congress, its loss of the confidence of this country and of Europe, the necessity for an executive ministry, and stated that the time was past to indulge in hopes of foreign aid. The States must depend upon themselves, and their only hope lay in a National Bank. There had been some diffidence in his previous letter. There was none in this, and he had a greater mastery of the subject. In something like thirty pages of close writing, he lays down every law, extensive and minute, for the building of a National Bank, and not the most remarkable thing about this letter is the psychological knowledge it betrays of the American people. Having despatched it, he wrote again to Washington, demonstrating that his case was dissimilar from those the Chief had quoted. He disposed of each case in turn, and his presentation of his own claims was equally unanswerable. Washington, who was too wise to enter into a controversy with Hamilton's pen, did not reply to the letter, but made up his mind to do what he could for him, although still determined there should be no disaffection in the army of his making.

Meanwhile Hamilton received letters from Lafayette, begging him to hasten South and share his exile; from Washington, asking advice; and from members of the family, reminding him of their affection and regret. Tilghman's is characteristic:—

Headquarters, 27th April.

> MY DEAR HAMILTON: Between me and thee there is a gulf, or I should not have been thus long without seeing you. My faith is strong, but not strong enough to attempt walking on the waters. You must not suppose from my dealing so much in Scripture phrase that I am either drunk with religion or with wine, though had I been inclined to the latter I might have found a jolly companion in my lord, who came here yesterday. We have not a word of news.... I must go over and see you soon, for I am not yet weaned from you, nor do I desire to be. I will not present so cold words as compliments to Mrs. Hamilton. She has an equal share of the best wishes of

Your most affectionate

TILGHMAN.

The following was from Laurens:—

> I am indebted to you, my dear Hamilton, for two letters: the first from Albany, as masterly a piece of cynicism as ever was penned; the other from Philadelphia, dated the second March; in both you mention a design of retiring, which makes me extremely unhappy. I would not wish to have you for a moment withdraw from the public service; at the same time my friendship for you, and knowledge of your value to the United States, makes me most ardently desire that you should fill only the first offices of the Republic. I was flattered with an account of your being elected a delegate from New York, and am much mortified not to hear it confirmed by yourself. I must confess to you that at the present stage of the war, I should prefer your going into Congress, and from thence becoming a minister plenipotentiary for peace, to your remaining in the army, where the dull system of seniority, and the *tableau*, would prevent you from having the important commands to which you are entitled; but, at any rate, I will not have you renounce your rank unless you entered the career above mentioned. Your private affairs cannot require such immediate and close attention. You speak like a *paterfamilias* surrounded with a numerous progeny.

On the 26th of May he had an appreciative letter from Robert Morris, thanking him for his suggestions, and assuring him of their acceptability. He promises a bank on Hamilton's plan, although with far less capital; still it may afterward be increased to any extent.

The northern land was full of amenities, the river gay with pleasure barges. The French gardens about the Schuyler mansion were romantic for saunterings with the loveliest of brides; the seats beneath the great trees commanded the wild heights opposite. Forty of the finest horses in the country were in General Schuyler's stables, and many carriages. There was a constant stream of distinguished guests. But Hamilton, who could dally pleasurably for a short time, had no real affinity for anything but work. There being no immediate prospect of fighting, he retired again to the library and began that series of papers called *The Continentalist*, which were read as attentively as if peace had come. They examined the defects of the existing league of states, their jealousies, which operated against the formation of a

Federal government, then proceeded to enumerate the powers with which such a government should be clothed.

Hamilton did not wait with any particular grace, but even the desired command came to him after a reasonable period of attempted patience. At Washington's request he accompanied him to Newport to confer with Rochambeau. Although the Chief did not allude to Hamilton's last letter, their intercourse on this journey was as natural and intimate as ever; and Washington did not conceal his pleasure in the society of this the most captivating and endearing of his many young friends. After the conference was over, Hamilton returned to Albany for a brief visit, then determined to force Washington to show his hand. He joined the army at Dobbs Ferry, and sent the Chief his commission. Tilghman returned with it, express haste, and the assurance that the General would endeavour to give him a command, nearly such as he could desire in the present circumstance of the army, Hamilton had accomplished his object. He retained his commission and quartered with General Lincoln.

When Washington arrived at Dobbs Ferry and went into temporary quarters, he gave a large dinner to the French officers, and invited Hamilton to preside.

> His graceful manners and witty speeches provoked universal admiration [runs the pen of a contemporary]. He was the youngest and smallest man present. His hair was turned back from the forehead, powdered, and queued at the back. His face was boyishly fair, and lighted up with intelligence and genius. Washington, grave, elegant and hospitable, sat at the side of the table, with the accomplished Count de Rochambeau on his right. The Duke de Luzerne occupied a seat opposite. General Knox was present, and so was Baron Steuben.

Shortly afterward, Hamilton attended a council of war, at Washington's invitation. The squadron of De Grasse was approaching the coast of Virginia. For the second time, Washington was obliged to give up his cherished scheme of marching on New York, for it was now imperative to meet Cornwallis in the South. The Chief completely hoodwinked Clinton as to his immediate plans, Robert Morris raised the funds for moving the army, and Hamilton obtained his command. To his high satisfaction, Fish was one of his officers. Immediately before his departure for the South he wrote to his wife. He had attained his desire, but he was too unhappy to be playful. A portion of the letter is as follows:—

> A part of the army, my dear girl, is going to Virginia, and I must, of necessity, be separated at a much greater

> distance from my beloved wife. I cannot announce the fatal necessity without feeling everything that a fond husband can feel. I am unhappy;—I am unhappy beyond expression. I am unhappy because I am to be so remote from you; because I am to hear from you less frequently than I am accustomed to do. I am miserable because I know you will be so; I am wretched at the idea of flying so far from you, without a single hour's interview, to tell you all my pains and all my love. But I cannot ask permission to visit you. It might be thought improper to leave my corps at such a time and upon such an occasion. I must go without seeing you—I must go without embracing you:—alas! I must go.

The allied armies moved on the 22d of August and arrived within two miles of the enemy's works at York Town, on the 28th of September. Hamilton's light infantry was attached to the division of Lafayette, who joined the main army with what was left of his own. Laurens was also in command of a company of light infantry in the young French general's division. He had acquitted himself brilliantly in France, returning, in spite of all obstacles and the discouragement of Franklin, with two and a half million livres in cash, part of a subsidy of six millions of livres granted by the French king; but he felt that to be in the field again with Washington, Hamilton, Lafayette, and Fish was higher fortune than successful diplomacy.

The allied army was twelve thousand strong; Cornwallis had about seventy-eight hundred men. The British commander was intrenched in the village of York Town, the main body of his troops encamped on the open grounds in the rear. York Town is situated on a peninsula formed by the rivers York and James, and into this narrow compass Cornwallis had been driven by the masterly tactics of Lafayette. The arrival of De Grasse's fleet cut off all hope of retreat by water. He made but a show of opposition during the eight days employed by the Americans in bringing up their ordnance and making other preparations. On the 9th the trenches were completed, and the Americans began the bombardment of the town and of the British frigates in the river. It continued for nearly twenty-four hours, and so persistent and terrific was the cannonading, that the British, being unfortunate in their embrasures, withdrew most of their cannon and made infrequent reply. On the night of the 11th new trenches were begun within two and three hundred yards of the British works. While they were completing, the enemy opened new embrasures, from which their fire was far more effective than at first. Two redoubts flanked this second parallel and desperately annoyed the men in the trenches. It was determined to carry them by assault, and the American light infantry and De Viomenil's grenadiers and chasseurs were ordered to hold themselves in readiness for the attack. Laurens, with eighty men, was to turn the redoubt in order to intercept the retreat of the garrison, but Hamilton, for the moment, saw his long-coveted opportunity glide by him. Washington had determined to give it to our hero's old Elizabethtown tutor, Colonel Barber, conceiving that the light infantry which had made the Virginia campaign was entitled to precedence. Hamilton was standing with Major Fish when the news of this arrangement was brought to him. He reached the General's tent in three bounds, and poured forth the most impetuous appeal he had ever permitted himself to launch at Washington. But he was terribly in earnest, and the prospect of losing this magnificent opportunity tore down the barriers of his self-possession. "It is my right to attack, sir!" he concluded passionately, "I am the officer on duty!" Washington had watched his flushed nervous face and flashing eyes, which had far more command in their glances than appeal, and he never made great mistakes: he knew that if he refused this request, Hamilton never would forgive him.

"Very well," he said. "Take it."

Hamilton ran back to Fish, crying: "We have it. We have it;" and immediately began to form his troops. The order was issued to advance in two columns, and after dark the march began, Hamilton leading the advance corps. The French were to attack the redoubt on the right.

The signal was a shell from the American batteries, followed by one from the French. The instant the French shell ascended, Hamilton gave the order to advance at the point of the bayonet; then his impatience, too long gnawing at its curb, dominated him, and he ran ahead of his men and leaped to the abatis. For a half moment he stood alone on the parapet, then Fish reached him, and together they encouraged the rest to come on. Hamilton turned and sprang into the ditch, Fish following. The infantry was close behind, and surmounting the abatis, ditch, and palisades, leaped into the work. Hamilton had disappeared, and they feared he had fallen, but he was investigating; he suddenly reappeared, and formed the troops in the redoubt. It surrendered almost immediately. The attack took but nine minutes, so irresistible was the impetuosity of the onslaught. Hamilton gave orders at once to spare every man who had ceased to fight. When Colonel Campbell advanced to surrender, one of the American captains seized a bayonet and drew back to plunge it into the Englishman's breast. Hamilton thrust it aside, and Campbell was made prisoner by Laurens. Washington was delighted. "Few cases," he said, "have exhibited greater proofs of intrepidity, coolness, and firmness than were shown on this occasion." On the 17th, when Washington received the proposition for surrender from Cornwallis, he sent for Hamilton and asked his opinion of the terms. To Laurens was given the honour of representing the American army at the conference before the surrender. Tilghman rode, express haste, to Philadelphia with the first news of the surrender of Cornwallis and his army.

Hamilton's description of his part in the conquest that virtually put an end to the war is characteristic.

> Two nights ago, my Eliza [he wrote], my duty and my honour obliged me to take a step in which your happiness was too much risked. I commanded an attack upon one of the enemy's redoubts; we carried it in an instant and with little loss. You will see the particulars in the Philadelphia papers. There will be, certainly, nothing more of this kind; all the rest will be by approach; and if there should be another occasion, it would not fall to my turn to execute it.
>
> "It is to be hoped so," she said plaintively to her mother. "Else shall I no longer need to wear a wig."

CHAPTER XII

The next few years may be passed over quickly; they are not the most interesting, though not the least happy of Hamilton's life. He returned home on furlough after the battle of York Town and remained in his father-in-law's hospitable home until the birth of his boy, on the 22d of January. Then, having made up his mind that there was no further work for him in the army, and that Britain was as tired of the war as the States, he announced his intention to study for the bar. His friends endeavoured to dissuade him from a career whose preparation was so long and arduous, and reminded him of the public offices he could have for the asking. But Hamilton was acquainted with his capacity for annihilating work, and at this time he was not conscious of any immediate ambition but of keeping his wife in a proper style and of founding a fortune for the education of his children. His military ambition had been so possessing that the sudden and brilliant finish at York Town of his power to gratify it had dwarfed for a while any other he may have cherished.

He took a little house in the long street on the river front, and invited Troup to live with him. They studied together. He had been the gayest of companions, the most courted of favourites, since his return from the wars. For four months even his wife and Troup had, save on Sundays, few words with him on unlegal matters. His brain excluded every memory, every interest. For the first time he omitted to write regularly to Mrs. Mitchell, Hugh Knox, and Peter Lytton. All day and half the night he walked up and down his library, or his father-in-law's, reading, memorizing, muttering aloud. His friends vowed that he marched the length and width of the Confederacy. He never gave a more striking exhibition of his control over the powers of his intellect than this. The result was that at the end of four months he obtained a license to practise as an attorney, and published a "Manual on the Practice of Law," which, Troup tells us, "served as an instructive grammar to future students, and became the groundwork of subsequent enlarged practical treatises." If it be protested that these feats were impossible, I can only reply that they are historic facts.

It was during these months of study that Aaron Burr came to Albany.

This young man, also, was not unknown to fame; and the period of the Revolution is the one on which Burr's biographers should dilate, for it was the only one through which he passed in a manner entirely to his credit. He was now in Albany, striving for admittance to the bar, but handicapped by the fact that he had studied only two years, instead of the full three demanded by law.

While Burr did not belong to the aristocracy of the country, his family not ranking by any means with the Schuylers, Van Rensselaers, Livingstons, Jays, Morrises, Roosevelts, and others of that small and haughty band, still he came of excellent and respectable stock. His father had been the Rev. Aaron Burr, President of Princeton College, and his mother the daughter of the famous Jonathan Edwards. He was quick-witted and brilliant; and there is no adjective which qualifies his ambition. He was a year older than Hamilton, about an inch taller, and very dark. His features were well cut, his eyes black, glittering, and cold; his bearing dignified but unimposing, for he bent his shoulders and walked heavily. His face was not frank, even in youth, and grew noticeably craftier. He and Hamilton were the greatest fops in dress of their time; but while the elegance and beauty of attire sat with a peculiar fitness on Hamilton, seeming but the natural continuation of his high-bred face and easy erect and graceful bearing, Burr always looked studiously well-dressed. In regard to their height, a similar impression prevailed. One never forgot Burr's small stature, and often commented upon it. Comment upon Hamilton's size was rare, his proportions and motions were so harmonious; when he was on the platform, that ruthless test of inches, he dominated and controlled every brain in the audience, and his enemies vowed he was in league with the devil.

Burr brought letters to General Schuyler, and was politely given the run of the library. He and Hamilton had met casually in the army, but had had no opportunity for acquaintance. At this time the law was a subject of common interest, and they exchanged many opinions. There was no shock of antagonism at first, and for that matter they asked each other to dinner as long as Hamilton lived. But Hamilton estimated him justly at once, although, as Burr was as yet unconscious of the depths of his own worst qualities, the most astute reader of character hardly would suspect them. But Hamilton read that he was artificial and unscrupulous, and too selfish to serve the country in any of her coming needs. Still, he was brilliant and fascinating, and Hamilton asked him to his home. Burr, at first, was agreeably attracted to Hamilton, whose radiant disposition warmed his colder nature; but when he was forced to accept the astounding fact that Hamilton had prepared himself for the bar in four months, digesting and remembering a mountain of knowledge that cost other men the labour of years, and had prepared a Manual besides, he experienced the first convulsion of that jealousy which was to become his controlling passion in later years. Indeed, he established the habit with that first prolonged paroxysm, and he asked himself sullenly why a nameless stranger, from an unheard-of Island, should have the unprecedented success which this youth had had. Social victory, military glory, the preference of Washington, the respect and admiration of the most eminent men in the country, a horde of friends who talked of him as if he were a demi-god, an alliance by marriage with the greatest family in America, a father-in-law to advance any man's ambitions, a fascination which had kept the women talking until he married, and finally a memory and a legal faculty which had so astounded the bar—largely composed of exceptional men—that it could talk of nothing else: it was enough for a lifetime, and the man was only twenty-five. What in heaven's name was to be expected of him before he finished? The more Burr brooded, the more enraged he became. He had been brought up to think himself extraordinary, although his guardian had occasionally birched him when his own confidence had disturbed the peace; he was intensely proud of his military career, and aware of his fitness for the bar. But in the blaze of Hamilton's genius he seemed to shrivel; and as for having attempted to prepare himself for practice in four months, he might as well have grafted wings to his back and expected them to grow. It was some consolation to reflect that, as aide and confidential secretary for four years to Washington, Hamilton had been a student of the law of nations, and that thus his mind was peculiarly fitted to grasp what confronts most men as a solid wall to be taken down stone by stone; also that himself acknowledged no rival where the affections of women were concerned. But while he lifted the drooping head of his pride, and tied it firmly to a stake with many strong words, he chose to regard Hamilton as a rival, and the idea grew until it possessed him.

In July Robert Morris, after some correspondence, persuaded Hamilton to accept the office of Continental Receiver for a short time.

> Your former situation in the army [he wrote], the present situation of that very army, your connexions in the state, your perfect knowledge of men and measures, and the abilities with which heaven has blessed you, will give you a fine opportunity to forward the public service.

Hamilton, who had no desire to interrupt his studies, was placed in a position which gave him no choice; his sense of public duty grew steadily.

> For my part [he wrote to Morris], considering the late serious misfortune to our ally, the spirit of reformation, of wisdom, and of unanimity, which seems to have succeeded to that of blunder and dissension in the British government, and the universal reluctance of these states to do what is right, I cannot help viewing our situation as

> critical, and I feel it the duty of every citizen to exert his faculties to the utmost.

But in spite of the onerous and disagreeable duties of his position, he continued to pursue the course of study necessary for admission to the bar as a counsellor. He also found time to write a letter to Meade. The following extract will show that the severity of his great task was over, and that he was once more alive to that domestic happiness to which so large a part of his nature responded.

> You reproach me with not having said enough about our little stranger. When I wrote last I was not sufficiently acquainted with him to give you his character. I may now assure you that your daughter, when she sees him, will not consult you about her choice, or will only do it in respect to the rules of decorum. He is truly a very fine young gentleman, the most agreeable in conversation and manners of any I ever knew, nor less remarkable for his intelligence and sweetness of temper. You are not to imagine by my beginning with his mental qualifications that he is defective in personal. It is agreed on all hands that he is handsome; his features are good, his eye is not only sprightly and expressive, but it is full of benignity. His attitude in sitting is, by connoisseurs, esteemed graceful, and he has a method of waving his hand that announces the future orator. He stands, however, rather awkwardly, and as his legs have not all the delicate slimness of his father's, it is feared he may never excel as much in dancing, which is probably the only accomplishment in which he will not be a model. If he has any fault in manners, he laughs too much. He has now passed his seventh month.

Happy by temperament, Hamilton was at this time happier in his conditions—barring the Receivership—than any vague, wistful, crowded dream had ever presaged. His wife was adorable and pretty, sprightly and sympathetic, yet accomplished in every art of the Dutch housewife; and although he was far too modest to boast, he was privately convinced that his baby was the finest in the Confederacy. He had a charming little home, and Troup, the genial, hearty, and solid, was a member of it. In General and Mrs. Schuyler he had found genuine parents, who strove to make him forget that he had ever been without a home. He had been forced to refuse offers of assistance from his father-in-law again and again. He would do nothing to violate his strong sense of personal independence; he had half of the arrears of his pay, Troup his share of the expenses of the little house. He knew that in a short time he should be making an income. The cleverest of men, however, can be hoodwinked by the subtle sex. The great Saratoga estate of the Schuylers furnished the larder of the Hamiltons with many things which the young householder was far too busy to compare with his slender purse.

He heard constantly from his friends in the army, and finally was persuaded to sit for a portrait, to be the common property of six or eight of them. Money was desperately tight, they could not afford a copy apiece, but each was to possess it for two months at a time so long as he lived; he who survived the others to dispose of it as he chose. For Hamilton to sit still and look in one direction for half an hour was nothing short of misery, even with Betsey, Troup, and the Baby to amuse him; and only the head, face, stock, and front of the coat were finished. But the artist managed to do himself justice with the massive spirited head, the deep-set mischievous eyes, whose lightnings never were far from the surface; the humour in the remarkable curves of the mouth, the determination and suppressed energy of the whole face. It was a living portrayal, and Betsey parted from it with tears. When she saw it again her eyes were dim with many tears. The last of its owners to survive fell far into poverty, and sold it to one of her sons. It is to-day as fresh, as alive with impatient youth and genius, as when Hamilton estimated portrait painters thieves of time.

Meanwhile a compliment was paid to him which upset his plans, and placed him for a short time in the awkward position of hesitating between private desires and public duty: he was elected by the New York legislature, and almost unanimously, a delegate to Congress. Troup brought him the news as he was walking on the broad street along the river front, muttering his Blackstone, oblivious of his fellow-citizens.

"Go to Congress!" he exclaimed. "Who goes to that ramshackle body that is able to keep out of it? Could not they find someone else to send to distinguish himself by failure? I've my living to make. If a man in these days manages to support his wife and child, there is nothing else he can do which so entitles him to the esteem of his fellow-citizens."

"True," said Troup, soothingly; "there certainly is nothing in that body of old women and lunatics, perpetually bickering with thirteen sovereign, disobedient, and jealous States, to tempt the ambition of any man; nor, ordinarily, to appeal to his sense of usefulness. But just at present there are several questions before it with which it is thought you can cope more successfully than any man living. So I think you ought to go, and so does General Schuyler. I know all that you will sacrifice, domestic as well as pecuniarily—but remember, you solemnly dedicated yourself to the service of this country."

"I'm not likely to forget it, and I am willing to sacrifice anything if I am convinced of my usefulness in a given direction, but I see no chance of accomplishing aught in Congress, of doing this country any service until it is a nation, not a sack of scratching cats."

Not only was great pressure brought to bear upon him, but he was not long convincing himself that it was his duty to take his knowledge of certain subjects vexing the Confederation, to the decrepit body which was feebly striving to save the country from anarchy. He had given little attention to the general affairs of the country during the past six months, but an examination of them fired his zeal. He accepted the appointment, and returned to his law books and his dispiriting struggle with the taxes.

In the autumn Hamilton received the second of those heavy blows by which he was reminded that in spite of his magnetism for success he was to suffer like other mortals. Laurens was dead—killed in a petty skirmish which he was so loath to miss that he had bolted to it from a sick-bed. Hamilton mourned him passionately, and never ceased to regret him. He was mercurial only among his lighter feelings. The few people he really loved were a part of his daily thoughts, and could set his heartstrings vibrating at any moment. Betsey consoled, diverted, and bewitched him, but there were times when he would have exchanged her for Laurens. The perfect friendship of two men is the deepest and highest sentiment of which the finite mind is capable; women miss the best in life.

In October Hamilton resigned the Receivership, having brought an honourable amount of order out of chaos and laid down the law for the guidance of future officials. November came, and he set off for Philadelphia philosophically, though by no means with a light heart. The baby was too young to travel; he was obliged to send his little family to General Schuyler's, with no hope of seeing them again for months, and a receding prospect of offering them a home in New York. His father-in-law, not unmindful that consolation was needed, drove him two-thirds of the distance, thus saving him a long ride, or its alternative, the heavy coach. In Philadelphia he found sufficient work awaiting him to drive all personal matters out of his head.

It was during this year of hard work and little result that he renewed an acquaintance with James Madison, Jr., afterward fourth President of the United States, and Gouverneur Morris, one of the most brilliant and disinterested young men in the country, now associated with Robert Morris in the Department of Finance. With the last the acquaintance ripened into a lifelong and intimate friendship; with Madison the friendship was equally ardent and intimate while it lasted. Madison had the brain of a statesman, energy and persistence in crises, immense industry, facility of speech, a broad contempt for the pretensions and mean bickerings of the States, and a fairly national outlook. As Hamilton would have said, he "thought continentally." But he lacked individuality. He was too patriotic, too sincere to act against his principles, but his principles could be changed by a more powerful and magnetic brain than his own, and the inherent weakness in him demanded a stronger nature to cling to. It happened that he and Hamilton, when they met again in Congress, thought alike on many subjects, and they worked together in harmony from the first; nevertheless, he was soon in the position of a double to that towering and energetic personality, and worshipped it. In their letters the two young men sign themselves, "yours affectionately," "yours with deep attachment," which between men—I suppose—means something. So noticeable was Madison's devotion to the most distinguished young man of the day, and a few years later so absorbed was he into the huge personality of his early friend's bitterest enemy, that John Randolph once exclaimed in wrath, "Madison always was some great man's mistress—first Hamilton's, then Jefferson's:" a remark which was safe in the days of our ancestors, when life was all work and no satiety.

Gouverneur Morris had sacrificed home, inheritance, and ties in the cause of the Revolution, most of his family remaining true to the crown. His education was thorough, however, and subsequently he had nine years of Europe, of which he left to posterity an entertaining record. Tall, handsome, a wit, a beau, notable for energy in Congress, erratic, caustic, cynical, but the warmest of friends, he was a pet of society, a darling of women, and trusted by all men. He and Hamilton had much in common, and to some degree he took Laurens's place; not entirely, for Laurens's idealism gave him a pedestal in Hamilton's memory which no other man but Washington ever approached; and Morris was brutal in his cynicism, placing mankind but a degree higher than the beasts of the forest. But heart and brain endeared him to Hamilton, and no man had a loftier or more burning patriotism. As for himself, he loved and admired Hamilton above all men. He was as strong in his nationalism, believing Union under a powerful central government to be the only hope of the States. Both he and Madison were leaders; but both, even then, were willing to be led by Hamilton, who was several years their junior.

The three young enthusiasts made a striking trio of contrasts as they sat one evening over their port and walnuts in a private room of a coffee-house, where they had met to discuss the problems convulsing the unfortunate country. Madison had the look of a student, a taciturn intellectual visage. He spoke slowly, weightily, and with great precision. Morris had, even then, an expression of cynicism and contempt on his handsome bold face, and he swore magnificently whenever his new wooden leg interfered with his comfort or dignity. Hamilton, with his fair mobile face, powerful, penetrating, delicate, illuminated by eyes full of fire and vivacity, but owing its chief attraction to a mouth as sweet as it was firm and humorous, made the other men look almost heavy. Madison was carelessly attired, the other two with all the picturesque elegance of their time.

"A debt of $42,000,000," groaned Morris, "interest $2,400,000; Robert Morris threatening to resign; delirious prospect of panic in consequence; national spirit with which we began the war, a stinking wick under the tin extinguisher of States' selfishness, stinginess, and indifference—caused by the natural reversion of human nature to first principles after the collapse of that enthusiasm which inflates mankind into a bombastic pride of itself; Virginia pusillanimous, Rhode Island an old beldam standing on the village pump and shrieking disapproval of everything; Jay, Adams, and Franklin, after years of humiliating mendicancy, their very hearts wrinkled in the service of the stupidest country known to God or man, shoved by a Congress not fit to black their boots under the thumb of the wiliest and most disingenuous diplomatist in Europe—much France cares for our interests, provided we cut loose from Britain; Newburg address and exciting prospect, in these monotonous times, of civil war, while peace commission is sitting in London; just demands of men who have fought, starving and naked, for a bare subsistence after the army disbands, modest request for arrears of pay,—on which to relieve the necessities of their families turned out to grass for seven years,—pleasantly indorsed by the Congress, which feels safe in indorsing anything, and rejected by the States, called upon to foot the bill, as a painful instance of the greed and depravity of human nature—there you are: no money, no credit, no government, no friends,—for Europe is sick of us,—no patriotism; immediate prospects, bankruptcy, civil war, thirteen separate meals for Europe. What do you propose, Hamilton? I look to you as your Islanders flee to a stone house in a hurricane. You are an alien, with no damned state roots to pull up, your courage is unhuman, or un-American, and you are the one man of genius in the country. Madison is heroic to a fault, a roaring Berserker, but we must temper him, we must temper him; and meanwhile we will both defer to the peculiar quality of your mettle."

Madison, who had not a grain of humour, replied gravely, his rich southern brogue seeming to roll his words down from a height: "I have a modest hope in the address I prepared for the citizens of Rhode Island, more in Hamilton's really magnificent letter to the Governor. Nothing can be more forcible—nay, beguiling—than his argument in that letter in favour of a general government independent of state machinery, and his elaborate appeal to that irritating little commonwealth to consent to the levying of the impost by Congress, necessary to the raising of the moneys. I fear I am not a hero, for I confess I tremble. I fear the worst. But at all events I am determined to place on record that I left no stone unturned to save this miserable country."

"You will go down to posterity as a great man, Madison, if you are never given the chance to be one," replied the father of American humour and coinage; "for it is not in words but in acts that we display the faith that is not in us. Well, Hamilton?"

"I must confess," said Hamilton, "that Congress appears to me, as a newcomer, rooted contentedly to its chairs, and determined to do nothing, happy in the belief that Providence has the matter in hand and but bides the right moment to make the whole world over. But I see no cause to despair, else I should not have come to waste my time. I fear that Rhode Island is too fossilized to listen to us, but I shall urge that we change the principle of the Confederation and vote to make the States contribute to the general treasury in an equal proportion to their means, by a system of general taxation imposed under continental authority. If the poorer States, irrespective of land and numbers, could be relieved, and the wealthier taxed specifically on land and houses, the whole regulated by continental legislation, I think that even Rhode Island might be placated. It may be that this is not agreeable to the spirit of the times, but I shall make the attempt—"

"Considering there is no spirit *in* the times, we might as well expect to inform its skull with genius by means of a lighted candle. You think too well of human nature, my boy; expect nothing, that ye be not disappointed, especially in the matter of revenue."

"I have no exalted opinion of human nature, but if I did not think more hopefully of it than you do, I should yield up that enthusiasm without which I can accomplish nothing. You have every gift, but you will end as a dilettante because your ideal is always in the mud; and it is only now and again that you think it worth while to pick it up and give it a bath."

"Right, right," murmured Morris, good-naturedly. "Would that I had your unquenchable belief in the worth while. Allied to your abilities it will make the new world over and upset the wicked plans of the old. Analyst and disbeliever in man's right to his exaggerated opinion of himself, how do you keep enthusiasm abreast with knowledge of human kind? Tell me, Hamilton, how do you do it?"

"I fear 'tis the essence of which I am made. My energies will have outlet or tear me to pieces. When there is work to do, my nostrils quiver like a war-horse's at the first roar and smoke—"

"Your modesty does you infinite honour; the truth is, you have the holy fire of patriotism in an abnormal degree. I have it, but I still am normal. I have made sacrifices and shall make more, but my ego curls its lip. Yours never does. That is the difference between you and most of us. Hundreds of us are doggedly determined to go through to the bitter end, sacrifice money, youth and health; but you alone are happy. That is why we love you and are glad to follow your lead. But, I repeat, how can you labour with such undying enthusiasm for the good of human kind when you know what they amount to?"

"Some are worth working for, that is one point; I don't share your opinion of general abasement, for the facts warrant no such opinion. And the battle of ideas, the fight for certain stirring and race-making principles,—that is the greatest game that mortals can play. And to play it, we must have mortals for puppets. To create a new government, a new race, to found what may become the greatest nation on the earth,—what more stupendous destiny? Even if one were forgotten, it would be worth doing, so tremendous would be the exercise of the faculties, so colossal the difficulties. I would have a few men do it all; I have no faith in the uneducated. The little brain, half opened by a village schoolmaster, is pestilential; but in the few with sufficient power over the many,—from whom will be evolved more and more to rank with the first few,—in those I have faith, and am proud to work with them."

"Good. I'd not have a monarchy, but I'd have the next thing to it, with a muzzle on the rabble. Perhaps I, too, have faith in a few,—in yourself and George Washington; and in Madison, our own Gibraltar. But the pig-headed, selfish, swinish—well, go on with your present plans. 'Tis to hear those we met to-night, not to analyze each other. Tell us all, that we may not only hope, but work with you."

"The army first. If retirement on half pay is impossible, then full pay for, say six years,—and the arrears,—paid upon the disbanding of the army. Washington, by the exercise of the greatest moral force, but one, that has appeared in this world, has averted a civil war—I am persuaded that horror is averted, and I assume that the country does not care eternally to disgrace itself by letting its deliverers, who have suffered all that an army can suffer, return to their ruined homes without the few dollars necessary for another start in life. I have resigned my claim to arrears of pay, that my argument may not be weakened. Then a peace establishment. Fancy leaving our frontiers to the mercy of state militia! I shall urge that the general government have exclusive power over the sword, to establish certain corps of infantry, artillery, cavalry, dragoons, and engineers, a general system of land fortifications, establishment of arsenals and magazines, erection of founderies and manufactories for arms, of ports and maritime fortifications—with many details with which I will not bore you. I shall urge the necessity of strengthening the Federal government through the influence of officers deriving their appointment directly from Congress—always, always, the necessity of strengthening the central government, of centralizing power, and of putting the States where they belong. It is federation or anarchy. Then—moderate funds permanently pledged for the security of lenders. I have preached that since I have dared to preach at all, and that is the only solution of our present distress, for we'll never get another foreign loan—"

> "We've accepted your wisdom, but we can't apply it,"
> interposed Morris.
> "Our only hope lies in your national government—but
> go on."

"A moment," said Madison. "This, in regard to the peace establishment: Do we apply a war congress to a state of peace, I fear we shall too clearly define its limits. The States may refuse obedience, and then the poor invalided body will fall into greater disrepute than ever."

"I have thought of that," replied Hamilton, "and if the worst comes to the worst, I have a radical plan to propose,—that Congress publish frankly its imperfections to the country—imperfections which make it impossible to conduct the public affairs with honour to itself or advantage to the United States; that it ask the States to appoint a convention, with full powers to revise the Confederation, and to adopt and propose all necessary alterations—all to be approved or rejected, in the last instance, by the legislatures of the several States. That would be the first step toward a national government. With that, all things would be possible,—the payment of our foreign loan, of our army, duties on foreign goods, whi ch is a source of revenue to which they are incredibly blind; the establishment of a firm government, under which all will prosper that are willing to work, of a National Bank, of a peace army—"

"Of Utopia!" exclaimed Morris. "Hamilton, you are the least visionary man in this country, but you are God knows how many years ahead of your times. If we are ever on two legs again, you will put us there; but your golden locks will thin in the process, and that rosy boyish face we love will be lined with the seams of the true statesman. Only you could contemplate imbuing these fossilized and commonplace intellects, composing our Congress of the Confederation—mark the ring of it!—with a belief in its own impotency and worthlessness. You are not mortal. I always said it. When Duane gave me your letter to read, I remarked: 'He withdrew to heaven, and wrote that letter on the knee of the Almighty; never on earth could he have found the courage and the optimism.' No, Hamilton, I would embrace you, did my wooden leg permit me to escape your wrath, but I can give you no encouragement. You will fail here—gloriously, but you will fail. Mark my words, the army will go home cursing, and scratch the ground to feed its women. The States will have no peace establishment to threaten their sovereign rights, we will pay nobody, and become more and more poverty-stricken and contemptible in our own eyes, and in the eyes of Europe; we will do nothing that is wise and everything that is foolish—"

"And then, when the country is sick unto death," interrupted Hamilton, "it will awake to the wisdom of the drastic remedy and cohere into a nation."

"Query," said Madison, "would it not be patriotic to push things from bad to worse as quickly as possible? It might be a case of justifiable Jesuitism."

"And it might lead to anarchy and the jaws of Europe," said Hamilton. "It is never safe to go beyond a certain point in the management of human affairs. What turn the passions of the people may take can never be foretold, nor that element of the unknown, which is always under the invisible cap and close on one's heels. God knows I have not much patience in my nature, and I do not believe that most of my schemes are so far in advance of even this country's development; but certain lessons must be instilled by slow persistence. I have no faith in rushing people at the point of the bayonet in times of peace."

"I think you are right there," said Morris. "But mark my words, you'll propagate ideas here, and the result in time will be the birth of a nation—no doubt of that; but you must rest content to live on hope for the present. I was a fettered limb in this body too long. I know its inertia."

He knew whereof he spoke. Hamilton won little but additional reputation, much admiration, half resentful, and many enemies. The army went home unpaid; the peace establishment consisted of eighty men; little or nothing was done to relieve the national debt or to carry on the business of government. Even his proposition to admit the public to the galleries of Congress, in the hope of interesting it in governmental affairs, only drew upon him the sneer that he could go out on the balcony and make his speeches if he feared his eloquence was wasted. He was accused of writing the Newburg address inciting the officers to civil war, because it was particularly well written, and of hurrying Congress to Trenton, when threatened by a mutinous regiment. But he worked on undaunted, leaving his indelible mark; for he taught the States that their future prosperity and happiness lay in giving up to the Union some part of the imposts that might be levied on foreign commodities, and incidentally the idea of a double government; he proposed a definite system of funding the debts on continental securities, which gradually rooted in the common sense of the American people, and he inveighed with a bitter incisiveness, which was tempered by neither humour nor gaiety, against the traitorous faction in the pay of France. He dissuaded Robert Morris from resigning, and introduced a resolution in eulogy of Washington's management of his officers in the most critical hour of the Union's history. But his immediate accomplishment was small and discouraging, although his foresight may have anticipated what George Ticknor Curtis wrote many years later:—

> The ideas of a statesman like Hamilton, earnestly bent on the discovery and inculcation of truth, do not pass away. Wiser than those by whom he was surrounded, with a deeper knowledge of the science of government than most of them, and constantly enunciating principles which extended far beyond the temporizing policy of the hour, the smiles of his opponents only prove to posterity how far he was in advance of them.

The following extract from a letter of James M'Henry, Lafayette's former aide, and a member of the Congress, is interesting as a commentary on the difficulties of our hero's position while a member of that body.

> DEAR HAMILTON: The homilies you delivered in Congress are still remembered with pleasure. The impressions they made are in favour of your integrity; and no one but believes you a man of honour and of republican principles. Were you ten years older and twenty thousand pounds richer, there is no doubt but that you might obtain the suffrages of Congress for the highest office in their gift. You are supposed to possess various knowledge, useful, substantial, and ornamental. Your very grave and your cautious, your men who measure others by the standard of their own creeping politics, think you sometimes intemperate, but seldom visionary: and that were you to pursue your object with as much cold perseverance as you do with ardour and argument, you would become irresistible. In a word, if you could submit to spend a whole life in dissecting a fly you would be, in their opinion, one of the greatest men in the world. Bold designs; measures calculated for their rapid execution; a wisdom that would convince from its own weight; a project that would surprise the

people into greater happiness, without giving them an opportunity to view it and reject it, are not adapted to a council composed of discordant elements, or a people who have thirteen heads, each of which pay superstitious adorations to inferior divinities.

Adieu, my dear friend, and in the days of your happiness drop a line to your

M'HENRY

At the end of 1783 Hamilton was convinced that he was of no further immediate use to the country, and refused a reelection to the Congress, despite entreaty and expostulation, returning to the happiness of his domestic life and to his neglected law-books. The British having evacuated New York, he moved his family there and entered immediately upon the practice of his profession.